STUDENT EXCHANGE

SPINETINGLERS

#22

STUDENT EXCHANGE

M. T. COFFIN

AN AVON CAMELOT BOOK

This is a work of fiction. Names, characters, places, and incidents either are the product of the author's imagination or are used fictitiously. Any resemblance to actual events, locales, organizations, or persons, living or dead, is entirely coincidental and beyond the intent of either the author or the publisher.

AVON BOOKS
A division of
The Hearst Corporation
1350 Avenue of the Americas
New York, New York 10019

Copyright © 1997 by Mike Ford
Excerpt from *Gimme Back My Brain* copyright © 1997 by Robert Hawks
Published by arrangement with the author
Visit our website at **http://AvonBooks.com**
Library of Congress Catalog Card Number: 96-95088
ISBN: 0-380-78804-7
RL: 4.9

First Avon Camelot Printing: June 1997

CAMELOT TRADEMARK REG. U.S. PAT. OFF. AND IN OTHER COUNTRIES, MARCA REGISTRADA, HECHO EN U.S.A.

Printed in the U.S.A.

OPM 10 9 8 7 6 5 4 3 2 1

It was a few minutes after midnight, way past the time when I should have been asleep. Everyone else had gone to bed hours before, and the only noises in the house were the rattling of the furnace coming alive in the basement and the sound of Jake snoring away at the end of my bed, where he had stretched himself out. I rubbed his ears, and he quieted down again, rolling over so that his legs were straight up in the air.

What was keeping me awake at that hour was a book. Yeah, I know, kids are supposed to stay up late at night reading comics and horror novels and other forbidden stuff. But this was a real, honest-to-goodness book. It was called *Visitors from the Skies: True Accounts of Alien Landings on Earth.* I'd found it at the bookstore in the mall that afternoon. I was supposed to be buying new cleats for soccer, but I stopped into the bookstore first and never quite made it to the sporting goods store.

See, I'm really into science fiction and fantasy—movies, television shows, comics, anything at all. I especially like to read science fiction. I love all those books about different worlds and what everyone thinks are imaginary creatures. Only I'm not so sure they're all that imaginary. I mean, why shouldn't all kinds of weird things exist? We have junk like instant pudding and VCRs and other stuff that never seemed possible until someone figured out how to make it, right? And now it all seems really normal. No one thinks chocolate pudding in a box is strange. So why not aliens and monsters and who knows what else.

So anyway, I'm looking around for a new book to read. And sitting there on the shelf alongside the other books is this one. What I noticed first was the cover. It's got this picture of a round, silver ship with blue lights all over it, just like the spaceships you see in all the movies. The spaceship is hovering over a town, like it's waiting for everyone to fall asleep before it lands.

Something about that picture made chills run down my spine. I felt like I should pick up the book and read it right there in the store. It was almost like something was telling me that I'd need to know what was in the book. So I decided the cleats could wait and I used all of the money I'd made raking leaves that week to buy the book.

I started reading after dinner, which I could

2

barely eat because I wanted to get into the book so badly. It was really amazing. It was all about aliens from different worlds who have come to Earth over the years. And the really strange thing is that all the stories were true. The author had found all of these secret government files about the aliens, files that had been locked away for years and years in the basement of some old building somewhere.

I couldn't believe it. Apparently aliens had been coming to Earth for years, but the government didn't want anyone to know about it. So they collected all of these stories and then spent a lot of time telling everyone they were hoaxes. They said the spaceships were clouds, or weather balloons, or even big flocks of birds. They made everyone think that believing in UFOs was crazy.

My favorite story was about this little town in Massachusetts called Samuelstown. Partly I was interested because I live in Massachusetts, too, and it was cool to think that aliens had been walking around my state, even if it was way before I was born. But mostly the story was just really incredible.

According to the book, way back in 1933 a spaceship landed in Samuelstown. It was filled with aliens from Venus. Only no one knew they were aliens. The aliens disguised themselves so that they looked just like everyone else in the town. In fact, they looked so real that one of the aliens was even elected mayor of Samuelstown. Another one taught English at the high school. They even played cards and went to potluck dinners along with everyone else.

Then one night all of the aliens disappeared. They just vanished—and so did everyone who lived in the town. One morning everyone who lived in Samuelstown was gone. Well, not everyone. The only person left was a little seven-year-old girl named Ella Crowe. The state police found Ella running down a dirt road. She was crying and mumbling something about ships that could fly and people with shining eyes.

When the police calmed her down, she told them that the night everyone disappeared she'd had a dream about a big, glowing spaceship. Everyone in town was lined up outside it, including Ella. She couldn't see her parents, so she went up to the police chief to ask him what was happening. When he turned around to answer her, she saw that his eyes were a funny color—they were glowing bright blue. She ran away and hid in a corn field. She heard people calling for her, but something about their voices seemed wrong, so she stayed hidden. She watched as the spaceship lifted up into the air and flew away. She didn't remember anything after that.

When she woke up the next morning, she was in her own bed. She was still dressed and her muddy shoes were on the floor. She couldn't remember leaving the house the night before and she didn't know how her shoes got dirty. She got up and went looking for her mother and father, but the house was deserted. She ran through the whole town calling out to people, but everyone had disappeared. She ran and ran until the police found her, almost three miles from town.

When the government heard about Ella's story, they sent doctors to study her. They hypnotized her and asked her to describe the aliens. She couldn't described them except to say that they had shining blue eyes and that they all wore circular pendants around their necks. The pendants were made of some kind of metal, and had strange letters carved all around them. The book had a picture of one of the pendants that Ella had described. The doctors believed that she couldn't describe the aliens because seeing them had scared her too much.

According to the book, the government ordered Ella's file to be locked away forever. No newspaper stories about what happened in Samuelstown ever appeared, and anyone who asked about the town was told that everyone there had died from an epidemic of cholera. Ella was taken away to an asylum, and no one ever heard from her again. Samuelstown was even taken off all the maps made after 1933, so that after a couple of years very few people even remembered it had existed.

Out of all the stories, Ella's fascinated me the most. I couldn't stop thinking about it. I wondered what had happened to the people of Samuelstown. Where did the aliens take them? What did they do with them? How had the aliens walked around for so long without anyone noticing that they were different? There was no way aliens could be in my town and I wouldn't notice it.

While I was thinking about the story, there was a sudden flash of blue light outside my bedroom window. It was really quick, like lightning, but there was no thunder or rain afterwards. I thought maybe it was the light on a police car, but I couldn't hear a car or a siren. I jumped out of bed and ran to the window to see what had made the light.

I couldn't see anything outside in the darkness, but a few miles away there seemed to be something in the sky over the corn field by Mr. Anderson's farm. I only saw it for a second, a row of blue lights twinkling in the blackness of the night sky, and then it was gone, as though someone had blown out a candle.

I decided I'd been up too late reading, and that I'd been seeing things. The lights were just stars. Getting back into bed, I put my book down and turned off the light. Still, as I fell asleep, a voice in the back of my mind kept telling me that stars weren't blue.

2

The next morning I was exhausted from staying up so late reading about aliens. I didn't even hear my alarm clock go off, and slept way past the time when I should have gotten up. But then my mother came in and said really loudly, "James Andrew Garcia, you get up *now* and come down to breakfast." Whenever she uses my full name I know she means business. Groaning, I rolled over and opened my eyes.

"Come on, Jake," I said. "Time to rise and shine." Jake yawned, stretched his legs, then jumped off the bed and headed downstairs to his breakfast. I crawled out of bed and pulled on jeans and a shirt, wishing I was still asleep. I managed to make it to breakfast, but barely had time to wolf down my oatmeal and orange juice before I had to run out the door. As it was, I almost missed the school bus and had to sit with a second grader who had a runny nose and kept talking about a cartoon he'd seen about a billion times. By the time I got to my classroom, I knew it was going to be a bad day.

My fears were confirmed when I heard Sharon Duckweeder and Butch Smirdley telling loud, stupid jokes to anyone who would listen. Sharon and Butch were best friends, mainly because they were so disgusting that no one else wanted to be around them. They really enjoyed picking on other people. I couldn't help but think that if there were any aliens at Westview Elementary School, it was probably them.

"Hey, Garcia," Butch said as I sat down at my desk. "Comb your hair with an electric mixer this morning?"

"No, Smirdley, I just saw your face and this is how scared I got." I knew it wasn't very original, but I was too tired to think of anything better. Luckily, Butch had already moved on to his next victim, a skinny kid with tape around his glasses, and left me alone.

"What's the matter with you?" Sandy asked. "You look like you haven't slept at all." Sandy Taylor is my best friend. We've known each other since the first day of kindergarten, when we both told the teacher we hated vanilla wafers at cookie time and got sent home with notes to our parents saying we were difficult to deal with.

"I feel like I haven't slept at all," I said, putting my head on my desk. "I was up late reading."

"Well, I hope you were reading your history book," she said, grinning. "Because we have a test this morning."

"Oh, no," I groaned. "I totally forgot."

"It's all about the colonization of America," she said. "You know, how people settled in the United States from different countries like England and Ireland because of political problems there."

"Well," I said, yawning, "I was reading about people taking over the country all right. But the people I read about came from outer space, not England."

Sandy laughed. "I don't think that's going to help you," she said. "You have to learn to be a little more realistic." Sandy wants to be a teacher, and she studies all the time. She doesn't believe in things like aliens and monsters.

Sharon Duckweeder overheard our conversation and started teasing me. "What's the matter, James, did little green men from Mars invade your house and steal your history book?"

"Ha, ha, ha, Sharon," I said. "No, but it looks like some of them invaded your house and left you behind."

Sharon stuck her tongue out at me. I stuck my tongue out back, just as our teacher, Mrs. Weir, walked in. "James, that's enough of that," she said. "Apologize to Sharon." Sharon looked over at me and smiled sweetly. I glared back, hoping maybe I could send her telepathic messages telling her what

9

a jerk she was. But what I said was, "Sorry." *Great,* I thought, *the worst morning of my life keeps getting worse by the minute. I can't wait to see what's next.*

That's when I noticed that Mrs. Weir wasn't alone. Walking behind her was a girl. She had long blond hair, and she seemed a little taller than most of the girls in our class. She stood next to Mrs. Weir's desk and looked around, as if she were scanning the room or something.

"Can I have your attention, class," said Mrs. Weir. Everyone quieted down and looked at the new girl. "This is Marilyn Hagen. Marilyn is an exchange student from Norway. She'll be living here in Westview for the year so that she can see what life is like in the United States."

"Hello," said Marilyn. "It's a pleasure to be here." Her voice sounded a little funny, like she had an accent, or like she was speaking in a tunnel.

"Marilyn just arrived here last night," said Mrs. Weir. "She's going to need some help finding her way around and getting used to things. I hope all of you will make her feel very welcome."

Mrs. Weir showed Marilyn to an empty desk right next to mine. "James, since you and Marilyn will have the same classes, I think it would be nice if you took her around for the day."

Marilyn looked over at me and smiled. I tried to smile back, but I wasn't very thrilled about having to drag her around with me all day long. "I'd be

10

happy to, Mrs. Weir," I said, trying to sound enthusiastic.

A few minutes later the bell rang for first period, and everyone filed out into the hall. Marilyn walked beside me as we made our way through the throng of screaming kids to our history class. Sandy walked with us, and she and Marilyn talked.

"It must be hard being so far from home," said Sandy.

Marilyn nodded. "Yes," she said. "I miss my family and my friends. But I'm sure this will soon feel like home, too. Everyone seems so nice."

"I'd like to visit your home someday," said Sandy. "It seems so far away."

"Not so far," said Marilyn, looking at us. "You may get to go there sooner than you think."

We walked into Mr. Grant's history class and sat down. I hoped he would postpone the test because of Marilyn's arrival, maybe use the hour to talk about international relations or the history of Norway. But of course he didn't. After saying hello to Marilyn and showing us where Norway was on a map, he passed out the test and told us to get to work. He told Marilyn she didn't have to take it, but she said she'd like to try. I couldn't believe anyone would actually want to take a test, but she did.

As I sat looking at my test, the questions all seemed to blur together. What was the main reason the Puritans left England? *To get away from having*

11

to take tests, I thought to myself. I checked off the multiple choice boxes randomly, hoping I'd get at least some right just by guessing. I looked over at Marilyn. To my surprise, she was busily checking off answers on her paper.

When Mr. Grant called for us to switch papers with the person next to us, I handed mine to Marilyn and took hers. As Mr. Grant called out the answers, I was amazed to find that Marilyn had gotten all of them right. I, on the other hand, did miserably. Out of twenty questions, I only got four correct, and that was because of lucky guesses.

We handed the tests in, and Mr. Grant flipped through them. "Well," he said. "It looks as though our exchange student knows more about this country's history than those of you who actually live here. Marilyn and Sandy received the highest scores in the class. Good work, Marilyn. Good work, Sandy."

I knew Sandy was smart, but I thought it was weird that Marilyn knew so much about America. Marilyn looked down at her desk. "I have studied your country for many years," she said.

Then Mr. Grant looked at me and frowned. "James, you could learn a thing or two from Marilyn. Maybe you should study with her next time there's a quiz."

I could feel my face turning bright red as everyone in class laughed at me. I slumped down in my seat and tried to make myself invisible. I couldn't wait for class, the rest of the day, and my whole life, to be over. I just wanted to go home and be alone.

After history, we had math class. We were doing fractions, and Miss Louis was up at the board making numbers dance around as she multiplied and added numerators and denominators with her chalk. I tried to focus on what she was saying, but my mind was wandering all over the place. I was thinking about aliens with blue eyes and about little Ella Crowe. When Miss Louis suddenly called out my name, I had no idea what she had asked me.

"James, I asked you what the common denominator of one third and one quarter is," she said, staring at me expectantly.

My head filled with all kinds of information as I tried to think of the correct answer. I thought about what a designated hitter in baseball does. I thought about how to diagram a sentence. I even thought about how many aliens could fit inside an average spaceship. But I couldn't think about how to make fractions add up at all. I just sat there staring at the board, hoping the answer would come to me.

Then I heard Marilyn whispering to me. "Twelve," she said in a low voice.

"Um, I think it's twelve," I said.

Miss Louis beamed. "That's right," she said. "Thank you, James."

13

I turned and looked at Marilyn. "Thanks a lot," I said. "You saved my life there."

"That's okay," she said. "I'm good at math."

You seem to be good at everything, I thought to myself. I wondered where Marilyn had learned so much. I guessed schools in Norway must be a lot harder than the ones here.

After math class it was time for gym. Marilyn went with Sandy to the girls' gym, and I went to the boys', where we played basketball. Even there I wasn't able to enjoy myself. I'm a good soccer player, and I like baseball, but I'm not great at basketball, and the fact that I was tired didn't help any. When Bob Cunningham passed me the ball, I tried to shoot it towards the net, but Alex Simons grabbed it out of my hands and raced down the court to score for the other team. Because of my error, they won by one point.

"Nice job," Bob said. "Next time try to at least remember what team you're on. Or maybe Marilyn can show you how to play ball after she tutors you in history." All the guys laughed at me, and I went into the locker room and kicked the wall.

Afterwards, I met up with Sandy and Marilyn in the cafeteria for lunch. Not surprisingly, I found out that Marilyn had in fact scored the winning basket for her team. After buying milk, we picked out a table and sat down. Sandy and I unpacked our bag lunches, but Marilyn didn't have anything with her.

"Aren't you going to eat anything?" Sandy asked.

Marilyn shook her head. "No, thank you. I'm not very hungry right now. I'm still tired from my trip."

Marilyn leaned back. As she did, her sweater opened and a necklace came into view. She started to push it back inside her shirt, but not before Sandy caught a glimpse of it.

"Oh," said Sandy, "what a pretty necklace that is. Can I see it?"

Marilyn held up the pendant for Sandy to see. It was round, and looked like it was made of some kind of silver metal. There were little markings all around the edge.

"That's so pretty," said Sandy. "Is that writing Norwegian?"

"Um, yes, it is," said Marilyn. "Those are ancient runes. This is a good luck charm."

I was looking at the pendant as Sandy turned it in her hand. It looked familiar, but I couldn't imagine where I could have seen it before. "Can I see that?" I asked.

Marilyn leaned across the table. I wondered why she didn't just take the necklace off and hand it to me, but I didn't ask. I looked carefully at the marks carved into the surface. I had no idea what they meant.

15

"I think I've seen a pendant like this before," I said.

Marilyn laughed and shook her head. "I don't think so," she said. "This is a family heirloom. It was made many years ago in Norway."

The rest of the day went by pretty smoothly, although Marilyn showed no signs of slowing down. In science class she was able to explain to Mrs. Crux what happens when solids become gasses. In English she wrote a poem that made Mr. Langley cry. Every one of the teachers thought she was amazing. Next to her, I felt like a total idiot.

When school was over, Sandy and I offered to walk Marilyn home. "That's okay," she said. "It's pretty far, and I have some things to do first. Thanks anyway, though. I'll see you tomorrow. And thanks for showing me around."

She waved goodbye to us and started walking away. "There's something strange about her," I said to Sandy as soon as Marilyn was out of earshot.

Sandy laughed and punched me in the arm. "You just think she's cute," she said.

"No, really," I said. "I mean, don't you think it's strange that she knows all this stuff about everything?"

"She's just really smart," said Sandy. "Maybe if you studied a little harder you'd know the answers, too."

"Maybe," I said, but something was still bothering me.

I said goodbye to Sandy and got on the bus. When I got home, I dropped my books on the kitchen table and went upstairs to do my homework. I opened my math book and began to do the problems. But my mind wasn't on math.

I picked up *Visitors from the Skies* and flipped through it. I figured reading a little bit would put me in a better mood for doing my homework. The book fell open to the drawing of the pendant that little Ella Crow had described, the ones worn by the aliens that had invaded Samuelstown. I sat on the bed staring at it.

All of a sudden, a light went on in my head. I ran into the hall, grabbed the phone, and dialed Sandy's number.

"Hello?" she said. She sounded as if she had just walked in.

"Hi, it's me," I said. "You're never going to believe this, but I know where I've seen Marilyn's pendant before."

"What are you talking about?" Sandy said after I explained to her about the pendant and the book. "Marilyn's no alien."

"I'm telling you, the pendant she was wearing today is the same as the one the alien's wearing in this book," I said. I was trying not to sound crazy, but I knew Sandy didn't believe a word I was saying. I could practically see her on the other end, shaking her head at me as if I'd just told her that Santa Claus had slid down my chimney and was standing in my living room with all his reindeer.

"Marilyn's necklace is a family heirloom, James. I think reading that book of yours is doing something to your mind."

"Listen," I said, "I know it sounds nuts. But it all makes sense. I mean, if she's an alien, that could explain how she knows all the stuff that she does. She's probably been studying everything

18

there is to know about Earth so she can be ready when her people take over."

"Right," said Sandy. "The Norwegians are going to take over the planet. They're going to attack us with herring and make us their slaves."

"Not Norwegians," I insisted. "Martians, or Uranians, or Jupiterians, or whatever they're called. They're probably just waiting until the time is right to take over. It's just like what happened in Samuelstown."

"What's Samuelstown?" Sandy said.

I told her the story of Ella Crowe and how the aliens had taken it over. "And no one ever suspected," I said when I finished the story.

There was silence on the other end. "You'll believe anything, won't you," Sandy said. "You've been watching too many episodes of *The X Files.*"

"Why won't you believe me?" I asked.

"Because it's nuts," said Sandy. "Marilyn is not an alien. She's an exchange student. Just because she's a little bit different doesn't mean she's from outer space. If everybody who was different was an alien, you'd be the first one I'd nominate for a trip to the stars. Besides, remember the time you thought there was a government plot to brainwash the kids of America by sending secret messages through Saturday morning cartoons? You even wrote a letter to the people who make *Mighty Morphin' Power Rangers* accusing them of being spies."

19

"Okay," I said. "I admit that was a little off. But this is different."

"No, it isn't. It's just another one of your strange ideas. Now I have to go and do my homework. You'd better spend your evening reading something besides books about aliens. We're having a quiz tomorrow in English."

I hung up the phone, went back to my room, and flopped down on the bed. I knew Sandy was right. My whole idea about Marilyn being an alien *was* pretty far out, even for me. So she knew a lot about different things. So what? My imagination was really working overtime.

I opened my English book and started to read about verbs and adverbs. Pretty soon I'd forgotten all about Marilyn and her pendant as I tried to remember when to use *lie* and when to use *lay*. By the time I went to bed, I was already laughing at myself. How could I ever have thought Marilyn was from outer space?

The next day at school I took my seat and said good morning to Marilyn and Sandy. "Hi," said Sandy. "Did you work out the problem you were having last night?"

Marilyn looked at me. "Were you having trouble with an assignment?" she asked.

"Sort of," I said. "But I figured it out. It's okay now."

"Good," said Sandy. "Marilyn and I were just talking about the new Thrashing Melons video."

"It's really cool," said Marilyn. "All about being in space and stuff. There are these flying saucers and guys in really bizarre costumes."

"Do you like science fiction?" I asked.

"I like some of it," Marilyn said. "I think space travel is really interesting. I mean, it would be interesting if it really existed."

"Do you believe in aliens?" I asked her. Sandy scowled at me over Marilyn's shoulder, but I just shrugged. I couldn't help myself. Besides, she'd started it.

"I guess there could be aliens," she said thoughtfully. "After all, if we exist, why shouldn't other beings exist on other planets? But I don't believe all of those stories about aliens coming to Earth and trying to take over the world. I think people make up those stories just to get attention."

She changed the subject then, and started talking to Sandy about maybe going shopping over the weekend. I wondered why she was acting nervous. Then Mrs. Weir came in and I didn't have time to think too much about it before she started calling roll. Her eyes travelled up and down the rows as she marked who was present and who wasn't.

"Does anyone know where Ed Brogan is?" she asked, making a mark in her attendance book.

We all turned and looked at Ed's empty chair.

21

"I don't think he's sick," said Paul Jenkins. "I talked to him on the phone last night, and he seemed fine."

"That's odd," said Mrs. Weir. "I wonder where he is."

"Maybe he had to go somewhere," said Marilyn suddenly.

"Maybe," said Mrs. Weir. "But it's unusual that his parents didn't send a note or anything."

Just then there was a knock on the classroom door. Mrs. Weir went and opened it, and a boy walked in. He was very thin, and had longish black hair that came down past his collar. He was wearing a red sweater, and he carried a note, which he handed to Mrs. Weir.

"My name is Orents Slimel," he said. "I was told by Principal Mulgrew to come here and to give you this note." I noticed that his voice sounded sort of like Marilyn's, a little high and squeaky.

Mrs. Weir unfolded the note and read it. "Well," she said. "Now I guess we know where Ed Brogan is. Apparently, he's become an exchange student. It says here that he's gone to live in Norway for the year, and that Orents will be living here with the Brogans."

Orents smiled at Mrs. Weir. His teeth were very white, so white they almost didn't look real. "Yes," he said. "The Brogans are very nice, and I think I will like it here very much."

I thought it was strange that Ed hadn't told anyone that he was going to be an exchange student. It didn't seem right that he would just leave without saying good-bye.

Orents went and sat in Ed's chair. As he passed Marilyn, I saw him smile at her. She returned the smile for a second, and I wondered if they knew each other, since they were both from Norway. I couldn't help but think that there was something odd about the way they looked at each other, as if they were sharing some kind of secret.

I didn't have a chance to talk to Sandy until lunch period. As soon as I entered the cafeteria she waved me over and I sat down.

"So what do you think of Orents?" she said.

I snorted. "Well, if you really want to know, I think he's kind of creepy. I didn't like the way he and Marilyn looked at each other."

"Oh, don't start that again," Sandy said. "I don't want to hear about the two of them being aliens or anything."

"I didn't say they were aliens, did I? I just said I think Orents is kind of creepy, and that he and Marilyn look like they're up to something."

"What could they be up to?" Sandy said. "They barely know their way around."

"Yeah, so why aren't they here then?"

Sandy looked around the cafeteria. Neither Or-

23

ents nor Marilyn was anywhere to be seen. "So they're not here. Maybe Marilyn is showing him around."

"I still say something weird is going on," I said. "I think after school we should go over and talk to Ed's parents."

"Okay, if it will make you feel better, I'll go," said Sandy. "But only because you're just going to look like a fool and I want to be there to tell you so."

After school I met Sandy on the front steps. She slung her backpack over her shoulder, and we started walking towards the Brogans' house.

"What are you going to ask them?" Sandy said.

"I guess I'll just ask how Ed is and why he didn't tell anyone he was going to Norway. Doesn't it seem strange to you that he would just suddenly up and go without telling *anyone?*"

"That is a little strange," Sandy admitted. "But maybe it was a last-minute thing, like he just found out and had to go."

"We'll see," I said. "Here's the house."

We walked up the path to the Brogans' front door and knocked. It opened, and Ed's mother was standing there. When she saw us, she smiled.

"Hello, James, how are you? I haven't seen you since the Scout picnic."

"Hi, Mrs. Brogan. This is my friend Sandy. We just stopped by to see how Ed is."

Mrs. Brogan smiled again. She seemed to be a little bit preoccupied, as though she was thinking about something else. "Why don't you come in?" she said. "I just made some chocolate-chip cookies."

Sandy and I walked into the house, and Mrs. Brogan shut the door. I had been in the Brogans' house a few times, and everything looked perfectly normal. I followed Mrs. Brogan into the living room, and Sandy and I sat on the sofa while she went to get the cookies.

"She's nice," Sandy said as soon as Mrs. Brogan was gone. "Think she's an alien, too?"

"Very funny," I said. "Look, I just want to find out what happened to Ed."

Mrs. Brogan returned with a plate of cookies and two glasses of milk on a tray. "Here we go," she said. "Help yourselves."

I took a cookie and ate it. "This is great," I said. It was true. The cookies tasted different than any I'd ever had before.

"They're Ed's favorites," said Mrs. Brogan, smiling again. I wondered why she kept smiling like that. It was weird. "I made a big box for him to take with him to Norway."

"We were really surprised to hear Ed had gone," I said. "He didn't tell any of us he was leaving."

Mrs. Brogan stared at me for a few seconds, as though she were thinking hard about something again. "Oh, it was all a big surprise," she said. "The exchange program people called yesterday and said there was an opening for Ed. He had to go right away or he'd lose his place."

I looked at Sandy. She was smiling back at Mrs. Brogan as though everything was perfectly fine. She took another cookie. She seemed to be enjoying them as much as I was. In fact, she seemed to be enjoying them a little too much. She'd already had four.

"I didn't know Ed even wanted to be an exchange student," I said. "He never mentioned it."

"Oh, Ed is very interested in foreign cultures," said Mrs. Brogan.

Something just wasn't right with the way Ed's mother was acting. It was as though everything she said was part of a script someone else had written, like the words were coming out of her mouth but she wasn't really saying them.

"So Orents is staying with you?" said Sandy.

Mrs. Brogan beamed at her. "Why, yes. Isn't Orents a sweet boy? We're so lucky to have him."

Sandy nodded. "He seems very nice," she said.

"So polite," said Mrs. Brogan, holding up the plate again. "Have another cookie."

Just then the front door opened and Orents came into the house. He looked at Sandy and I sitting on the couch, and for a moment it looked as though he frowned. Then the creepy smile I recognized from that morning returned, and he waved. "Hello there," he said, coming into the room. "Nice to see you two again."

"James and Sandy were just asking about you," said Mrs. Brogan.

Orents looked at me. "Oh, really? What would you like to know?"

"I was just asking Mrs. Brogan how you liked living here," I said.

"Oh, I like it just fine," said Orents. "I think it's going to work out very well."

I picked up the plate of cookies and held it out to Orents. "Would you like a cookie?" I asked.

Orents shook his head. "No, thank you, I'm not very hungry. In fact, I think I should go lie down for a while. I'm a little bit tired from my first day at school. It was nice to see you both."

"Goodbye," said Sandy. "See you tomorrow."

After Orents left, Sandy and I said goodbye to Mrs. Brogan. When we were back on the street, Sandy turned to me. "See?" she said. "Everything's fine."

"Everything is not fine," I said. "Didn't you notice how oddly Mrs. Brogan was behaving?"

"I think she was very nice," said Sandy. "Her cookies were delicious." Sandy seemed to be preoccupied with something. And she kept smiling.

"Something's wrong," I said. "And Orents seemed really annoyed to find us there. But the cookies were good. I sort of wish I had another one right now."

"He seemed perfectly normal to me," said Sandy.

We were walking through the Brogans' backyard, taking a shortcut to my street. As we passed a big oak tree, I noticed something on the ground. Walking over to the tree, I picked up a piece of material that was partially covered by leaves.

"What's that?" asked Sandy.

I held it up. It was a blue and green baseball jacket. "It's Ed's," I said, a horrible thought beginning to fill my mind. "It's his favorite jacket. He never goes anywhere without it."

Sandy looked doubtfully at the jacket in my hand. "You're sure that it's Ed's?"

I turned the jacket over and showed her where Ed's name was stitched across the front in white letters. "See? He wore it every day. There's no way he would have left it behind, especially outside. Something really awful must have happened to him."

"But why would Mrs. Brogan tell us everything is fine? That doesn't make any sense." Sandy seemed to be having a hard time thinking. She kept rubbing her head.

"I don't know," I said. "Nothing is fitting together. But I just know it has something to do with Marilyn and Orents."

This time Sandy didn't say anything. She just had a strange look on her face.

"What's the matter?" I asked.

She frowned. "I feel weird," she said. "Sometimes what you're saying makes sense, and sometimes it

doesn't. Maybe I'm coming down with something."
She shook her head. "There has to be some rational
explanation for all of this," she said. "We just have
to figure out what it is."

I started to walk away. "Fine, when you figure it
out, you let me know. In the meantime, I'm going
to find out more about our alien visitors."

Sandy ran up behind me. "Wait a second," she
said, grabbing my arm. "Don't be mad. I just meant
that there's probably a normal, everyday reason
why Ed left his jacket behind. If someone had kidnapped him or something, don't you think they'd
have done a better job of hiding the evidence?"

"Probably," I agreed. "That is, unless he hid it
there on purpose so someone would find it."

Sandy and I looked at each other for a minute.
She seemed to be thinking. "This is all too strange,"
she said finally. "I can't think about it clearly. Besides, I have to get home for dinner. Let's talk
about it more tomorrow."

"Okay," I said. "That is, if we're around
tomorrow."

Sandy laughed. "Hey, I'll let you know if I plan
on becoming an exchange student."

The next day my mother surprised me with a trip
to the dentist for a teeth cleaning, and I got to
school just in time for gym class. When I ran into
the locker room, I saw Orents suiting up.

"Hi, James," he said, his voice like ice-cold air in my ears. "It was . . . unexpected . . . to see you last night. Did you have a nice time talking with Mrs. Brogan?"

"Yeah, she's really great," I said, trying to sound casual. "Ed's a good friend of mine, you know."

"Really?" said Orents as he walked past me into the gym. "Maybe you'll get to see him soon." His voice sounded almost threatening, and I shivered.

When I finished dressing, I joined the other guys in the gym. We were playing basketball again, and they were choosing teams.

"I'll take Garcia," said Mitch Ballard, and I ran over to stand in his team.

Orents was one of the last guys chosen, and thankfully he was on the other team. The idea of having him on my team made my skin crawl, and I was glad to have him where I could keep an eye on him. I wasn't so happy, though, when Mitch assigned me to cover him.

The coach blew the whistle, and we started playing. Mitch, who was playing center, tipped the ball towards me. I grabbed it out of the air and started down the court. The way was clear, and I thought I had a straight run to the basket. If I made it, I'd make up for losing the game on Tuesday.

I was just about to go into my lay-up when I felt something smash into me. I fell down hard on the

31

court. The breath was knocked out of me, and for a moment all I could do was stare up at the ceiling.

Then I saw someone looking down at me. It was Orents, and he was smiling. "I'm so sorry," he said in his thin voice. He didn't sound like he was at all sorry. In fact, he sounded like he'd done it on purpose.

He held out one thin hand and grabbed mine. As he pulled me to my feet, I noticed something on his shirt. Hanging around his neck was a pendant, and it looked exactly like the one Marilyn wore. My eyes must have widened, because suddenly Orents looked down. When he saw what I was looking at, he quickly stuffed the pendant back inside his T-shirt and turned around. I stared at his back as he walked away. Something was definitely up, and I wanted to know what it was.

The rest of the gym period went by in a haze. My mind was filled with all kinds of thoughts about Marilyn and Orents and what might have happened to Ed. I couldn't wait to find Sandy and talk to her. That didn't stop me, though, from making three baskets and preventing Orents from making any. If he wanted a fight, I was going to give it to him.

I found Sandy in our usual lunch place.

"Hey, where have you been all day?"

"Dentist," I said. "My mom thought my teeth needed a good spit shine."

Sandy made a face. "Gross," she said.

I grinned at her, showing my newly-whitened chompers. "That's not the big news of the day, though. Guess what I found out?"

I told Sandy all about my run-in with Orents, and about the pendant. "It's exactly like Marilyn's," I said triumphantly. I waited for her to admit that I'd been right all along.

Instead, she took another bite of her sandwich, chewed it, and swallowed. "Okay," she said finally. "So they have the same pendant. But if it's an ancient Norwegian good luck charm, then doesn't that make sense?"

I couldn't believe she was being so dense. Couldn't she see that all of the pieces fit perfectly?

"What else do you need?" I said. "For a spaceship to land in front of your house and aliens to knock on the door?"

"That would be a start," she said.

"But what about Ed's jacket?"

"I've been thinking about that," she said. "Last night my head felt funny, and nothing made sense. But then it cleared. Isn't it possible that he left it on top of his luggage to take to the airport and that it simply fell off the pile?"

I thought about it. "I suppose that *could* have happened," I admitted. "But I doubt it. It was all covered with leaves. You saw it."

"It was really windy the other night," she pointed out. "The leaves could have blown over it."

I sighed. Every time I thought I had Sandy convinced that aliens were taking over our school, she came up with some other explanation.

"You win," I said. "Everything is fine. Marilyn and Orents are just two kids from Norway. Ed Brogan just decided at the last minute to become an exchange student. Nothing weird is going on at all. I'm just crazy."

"Thank you for admitting it," said Sandy sweetly. "Are you going to eat that cookie?"

I handed her the cookie and started to eat my sandwich. I had to think of a way to get Sandy to believe me.

"Hey," Sandy said, interrupting my thoughts. "Did I tell you I'm having a slumber party tomorrow night?"

"Big thrill," I said. "A bunch of girls sitting around talking about boys and combing their hair. Sorry I can't be there."

"That's not all we do," Sandy said. "We eat, too. Anyway, I've invited Marilyn to come."

"Great," I said. "Why not just invite every Venusian in town over while you're at it."

"It will be fun," Sandy said, ignoring me. "Maybe if you got to know Orents better you'd understand more about his culture."

"I saw *Star Wars* twelve times," I said. "I know all about what aliens do. I don't need to know any of them personally."

"You're hopeless," said Sandy.

*   *   *

Saturday was spent going with my parents to visit my Aunt Ruth, who always pinches my cheeks and tells me I look just like my dad. I was too busy trying to keep out of range of her fingers to think about Marilyn and Orents. But that night after dinner I opened *Visitors from the Skies* again, to see if I could find out any more about the aliens that had invaded Samuelstown. I looked at the drawing of the pendant again and again. The more I looked at it, the more I was convinced that it was the same as the ones that Marilyn and Orents wore. I looked for information about the pendants in the text.

> *Although Ella Crowe was able to describe the pendants worn by the aliens very clearly, she said she had no idea what they were used for. It is theorized that they serve as some kind of identification, a way for aliens of various races to tell one another apart. This is, however, merely a theory, as no other clues as to their purpose have been found.*

I closed the book and thought. If Marilyn and Orents were aliens, what were they doing in Westview? And what did they want with a bunch of kids? Where was Ed Brogan, and why was his mother acting so odd?

There were so many unanswered questions and

so many things to think about, I didn't know where to start. Even my best friend didn't believe me. In fact, right at that moment she was probably braiding an alien's hair and telling it her deepest secrets. I felt totally helpless. I flipped on the television and watched a *Star Trek: The Next Generation* rerun. Sometime during the show, I fell asleep.

What seemed like only a few minutes later, I woke up to the sound of ringing. It was the telephone. I ran into the hallway and picked up the phone. "Hello?"

"It's me," said Sandy. She sounded scared.

"What's wrong?" I asked. "It's like two in the morning or something."

"It's five after six," she said. "I waited as long as I could. I would have called you earlier, but I was afraid your parents would answer."

"What's going on? You sound freaked."

"I am," she said. "Something really strange is going on."

"Thanks for noticing," I said sarcastically.

"No, really," Sandy said. "This is really scary now."

"Why are you whispering?" I asked.

"I don't want her to hear me," Sandy said. It sounded as though her hand was covering the receiver.

"Her who?"

"Marilyn," Sandy said. "She's in the next room with the other girls, sleeping. I snuck out so I could call you before they all wake up."

"What did she do?"

Sandy took a deep breath. "Okay, this is going to sound weird. Even weirder than some of the stuff you've been thinking. Last night was fine. We all sat around and watched a Julia Roberts movie."

"Sounds really spooky," I cracked.

"Just listen. Around two o'clock I woke up. I got up and went into the kitchen for a glass of water. I was getting my drink when I happened to look out the window. I saw someone in the back yard."

"Let me guess," I said. "It was Marilyn."

"I'm getting to that part," said Sandy impatiently. "The kitchen door was open, so I snuck out. I hid behind the big tree in the back."

"So what was going on?"

"Well, at first all I heard was this strange sound, like a lot of crickets chirping. Then there was quiet, and I heard the same thing again. Only this time it sounded farther away, like it was coming over the radio or something."

I was wide awake now as I listened to Sandy. I couldn't believe that while I'd been asleep she'd been having an adventure. "What was it?"

"It was Marilyn."

"Marilyn? What was she doing?"

"That's the best part," said Sandy. "She was talking into her pendant."

"You mean her ancient Norwegian charm," I said triumphantly.

"Okay, so maybe you were right about that. She was holding it up to her mouth and talking into it. Then she'd wait a minute and someone would talk back."

"Someone, or something," I said.

"Those pendants must be some kind of communication device," said Sandy. "Like radios or walkie-talkies."

"So who is she communicating with?"

Sandy was silent for a minute. "I don't know," she said finally.

"You probably don't want to," I said.

All of a sudden I heard noises on the other end of the phone.

"People are starting to wake up," Sandy said. "I have to go. We'll talk later after they all go home."

"What are you going to say to Marilyn?"

"Nothing. I'm going to pretend nothing is out of the ordinary. After I saw her I went back inside and pretended to be asleep. She came in a few minutes later and went to bed too."

"Well, call me as soon as you can," I said. "We have to make a plan."

"There's one more thing," Sandy said. "After she finished talking, Marilyn bent down and picked something off the ground and ate it."

"She ate grass?" I said, my stomach churning.

"No," said Sandy just before she hung up. "It was a worm."

5

The hours I spent waiting for Sandy to call back were some of the worst of my life. All I could do was sit in my room and think about what she had told me. Marilyn had been using her pendant to talk to someone. Did that mean the pendants were radios? How did they work? Most important, who was she talking to? I wasn't sure I really wanted to know the answer to that question. When I thought about her eating a worm, my stomach lurched.

While I was sitting and thinking, my father came in and asked me to rake up the leaves in the yard. For once I was glad to have a chore to do, because it kept me busy while I waited to hear from Sandy again. I attacked the leaves with the rake, working out my frustrations on them.

I had gotten almost all of the front yard swept into two neat piles when my mother called to me that Sandy was on the phone. I ran inside and upstairs.

"Okay, what happened?" I said, hardly able to breathe.

"Nothing happened," Sandy said. "We all got up, had breakfast, and then everybody went home. Marilyn thanked my mother for having her, and even gave her a box of Norwegian chocolate. My mom thought she was really polite, and invited her over for dinner."

"She'd better serve worms," I said.

"Don't remind me," Sandy said. "At least you didn't have to see her swallow it. I thought I was going to be sick."

"What did you have for breakfast, spiders?"

"No, eggs and bacon. But Marilyn didn't have any. She said she wasn't hungry. She wouldn't even have any orange juice."

"I bet she wasn't hungry, after her midnight snack." I thought for a second. "You know, I've never seen Marilyn eat anything at all. Have you?"

"Just the worm," said Sandy.

"I mean real food. Orents never eats, either," I said. "Remember when Mrs. Brogan offered him the chocolate-chip cookie? He didn't take it."

"And they're never in the cafeteria at lunch," Sandy added. "What do you think it means?"

"I don't know," I said. "But it certainly is suspicious. I'm more interested in what she was doing outside."

"It really sounded like she was having a conver-

40

sation with someone," said Sandy. "But it didn't sound like any language I've ever heard. It sounded more like . . . insects or something. No, not quite insects, more like snakes. All I could hear was static."

"But you're sure she was talking into her pendant?"

"Yes, that much I saw clearly. She was holding it in her hand and talking into it. It must be some kind of a radio. So what do we do now?"

"I don't know," I said. "We can't tell anyone, because who would believe us? We need more proof. So now do you believe me?"

"Maybe," said Sandy. "Something strange is definitely happening here. I just don't know what it is."

I sighed. Sandy is always so stubborn. It's her scientific brain. "Well I for one want to find out," I said. "Meet me at the corner of Broward and Chestnut in fifteen minutes."

"Where are we going?"

"To find out where Marilyn really lives," I said.

I quickly gathered up some things I thought I'd need and stuffed them into my backpack. Then I went to meet Sandy. She was waiting when I got there.

"Okay, so what do we do?" she asked.

"I heard Marilyn tell Katherine Gleason that

41

she's living over near the cemetery," I said. "I think we should walk over there and see if we can find out which house she's living in."

"What good is that going to do?"

"I don't know," I said. "I just have a feeling it might tell us something about who, or what, she is."

We walked down the street to the far end of town. Our town isn't very big, so it wasn't long before we reached the area where Marilyn said she was living. She'd never said exactly *who* she was living with, so we didn't really know where to start looking. Sandy suggested we knock on doors and ask people if they knew where Marilyn was staying.

"We can pretend we're friends of hers from school or something," she said. "We can say we need to get an assignment from her."

We went up to the first house and knocked. A man answered, and we asked him if he'd seen Marilyn.

"I can't say that I have," he said. "But then I work most days and don't get home until late. If you find her, though, ask her if she's the one who's been setting off fireworks at night. Scares my dog half to death."

"Fireworks?" I said.

"Bright blue ones," the man said. "First ones were about a week ago. Saw them from my upstairs window when I was getting ready for bed. Saw 'em again a few nights ago. Made the whole house shake, too."

"I don't know about fireworks," I said. "But we'll be sure to ask her when we find her. Thanks for your help."

The man shut his door, and we walked down the street. Something he'd said about the fireworks was working around in my brain. Then I remembered.

"Those fireworks," I shouted. "I saw them, too. Only they aren't fireworks."

"What are you talking about?" Sandy said.

"The blue fireworks," I said. "The night before Marilyn arrived I saw blue lights floating over the field by the Anderson place. I bet those lights were what that man saw, too."

"Okay, so what do they mean?"

"Don't you see?" I said excitedly. "They weren't fireworks. They were lights from a spaceship. The spaceship that brought Marilyn here. And what shook the man's house was the spaceship landing."

Sandy's eyes grew huge as she realized what I was saying. I could tell even her scientific mind was believing my story now. "And if he saw the blue lights more than once . . . ."

"It means the ship has landed several times," I said, finishing her sentence. "That means there could be dozens of aliens running around."

Sandy and I stood looking at one another for a few minutes as we thought about what was hap-

43

pening. If a spaceship, or spaceships, had landed
several times already, there was no telling how
many aliens were living in Westview.

"We're the only ones who know," said Sandy.
"What are we going to do?"

"We have to think," I said. "But first I think we
should find out where Marilyn is. She seems to be
behind all of this."

We knocked on a few more doors on the street.
No one had seen Marilyn, but three other people
reported seeing the strange blue lights. One person
thought they were lights from a plane, another
thought they were fireworks like the first man had,
and the third person thought it was helium balloons that someone had let go.

"See why no one believes it when people report
seeing UFOs?" I said to Sandy. "Everyone likes to
think there's a reasonable explanation for strange
stuff."

Finally, at the last house we visited, a woman
said that she'd seen Marilyn. "Saw her the other
night," she said. "Thought it was odd, a young girl
walking by herself so late at night."

"Where did she go?" I asked.

The woman pointed towards an old abandoned
house sitting in a field. "Went that way," she said.
"Of course, she couldn't be living there. No running
water or electricity or anything. No one's lived

there for years. Not since old Mrs. Grundy died, anyway."

We thanked the woman for her help and started to walk towards the old house. It certainly looked as though it hadn't been lived in for a long time, but it was the only clue we had to go on. As we got nearer, I started to get a strange feeling in my stomach.

"I'm scared," I said to Sandy. "I don't know what's in there."

"Me too," agreed Sandy. "What are we going to do if she answers the door?"

"I think we should sneak around the back," I said. "That way we can look around without her seeing us. If she is some kind of alien, I don't want her to know that we know it."

There was a stand of pine trees running along one side of the old house. Sandy and I walked through them until we were near the back side of the house. There was a porch there, and a door. Peeking in a window, I saw a table and some chairs, and I could see a stove and a sink.

"It's a kitchen all right. But it looks like no one's been in it for years. Everything looks covered in dust."

"Try the door," she said.

I put my hand on the old doorknob and turned. To my surprise, the door opened easily. It swung inward, and Sandy and I stepped into the kitchen.

I started to sneeze, but was able to hold it in just in time so that it came out as a sort of squeak.

"It's dusty, that's for sure," I said.

"Look," said Sandy. "There's still a plate on the table." She went over and picked it up. There was a dried-up fried egg on it.

"Hard as a rock," Sandy said, tapping it with her fingernail. "It's been here for a long time."

On the other side of the kitchen was another doorway. I went over to it and looked through. Beyond it was what looked like a living room. Because the windows were boarded up, I really couldn't see very well. I opened my backpack and pulled out a flashlight. I switched it on and shined the thin yellow beam around the room. The circle of light revealed a couch, a chair, and an old radio, all of them covered with dust.

"Just old junk," I said. "This is a dead end—no one's here."

I was about to switch off the flashlight and leave when Sandy pointed to something. "What's that?" she asked.

I shined the light in the direction she was pointing. In the corner of the room there was a stairway going up to the second floor. In the dust that covered the floor were footprints leading from the front door to the foot of the stairs.

"Someone's been coming and going," said Sandy.

46

"And I bet I know who it is," I said. "Let's check upstairs."

As quietly as we could, we walked across the living room and started up the stairs. The stairway was black as night, and I wasn't too thrilled about going up it and running into who knew what. With each step the knot inside me tightened and told me to run out the back door and keep going until I got home. But I wanted to find out what was up there. Even though my stomach was clenched and my hands were shaking, I was determined to go up those stairs.

One by one, I went up the steps, with Sandy close behind me. My flashlight flickered on the walls as we ascended to the second floor, following the dusty footprints. At the landing, the footsteps disappeared down a hallway towards the back of the house.

Moving to the left, I entered what turned out to be a bathroom. I shined the light around on a toilet, a sink, and an old claw-foot bathtub. None of them seemed to have been used in a long time. There were spiderwebs in the bathtub, and I could see spiders scurrying around when I shined my light inside it.

"Whoever lives here sure doesn't worry about keeping clean," I whispered to Sandy.

Back in the hallway, I shined the flashlight's beam down the hall. It illuminated a few feet ahead of us, and then was swallowed up in darkness. Any relief I'd felt at finding the bathroom empty disappeared as I started down the hall.

The footprints went all the way to the end of the hall, then ended at a closed door. Sandy and I stopped there and looked at one another.

"What do you think is behind this?" I asked.

Sandy swallowed. "I guess we should find out," she said.

The door creaked slightly as I pushed it open and looked into the black mouth of the room. Inching inside, I shined the light around. There was a bed in the room—a big four-poster with some kind of curtains around it. The curtains seemed to be made out of a shiny material that glittered in the beam from the flashlight.

I turned around to motion to Sandy to come in. As I did, the flashlight illuminated something standing beside Sandy. Something with long blond hair.

"Marilyn!" I gasped.

Sandy spun around, ready to defend herself. But it wasn't Marilyn. It was just her head. And it was sitting on a long shelf. In fact, all along the shelf there was a row of heads, and all of them had Marilyn's face. Only there were no eyes in them.

"What are they?" Sandy said, backing away from the disembodied heads.

"I don't know," I said. I went closer and touched

48

one of them. The skin was rubbery, but also warm. "They're masks," I said. "Masks of Marilyn's face."

"Why would someone want so many masks?" Sandy asked.

I turned and looked at the bed. The curtains glowed softly in the light. "I'm not sure," I said. "But I have a feeling the answer is behind those curtains."

Walking over to the bed, I touched the curtains. They felt heavy and kind of slippery beneath my fingers, as though they were made of some kind of metal.

"Here goes nothing," I said to Sandy.

I slowly pulled back one of the side curtains. When I saw what was behind it, I almost screamed. Lying in the bed was Marilyn. She seemed to be sleeping, only she was covered by a plastic shield of some sort, and there were all kinds of blinking lights on it. There were tubes going into the shield, and glowing blue liquid was moving through them.

Sandy stepped in next to me and looked down at Marilyn. "Is she sleeping?"

"I guess so," I said. "But the question is, what is she? What are all of these tubes and lights and things?"

"It looks like some kind of life-support system," said Sandy, bending down to get a better look.

All of a sudden Marilyn opened her eyes. Only instead of human eyes, she had bright blue eyes with no centers. They looked like shining blue stars.

49

"Let's get out of here," I shouted, and started to run. Sandy was right behind me as I flew down the stairs, through the house, and out the back door, my feet barely touching the floor. As I ran for the cover of the pine trees I didn't even stop to turn around to see if the Marilyn creature was behind me. All I wanted to do was to get as far away from the thing in the bedroom as I could.

When I finally stopped to catch my breath, I looked for Sandy. She was running towards the trees, her breath puffing out in heavy clouds as she came to a stop next to me.

"Thanks for waiting," she said.

"Sorry," I said. "That thing really freaked me out. Did she follow us?"

"I don't think so," Sandy said. "I didn't hear anyone coming down the stairs after us. All the same, I think we should get out of here as soon as we can. I certainly don't want to be out here at night with whatever that thing was walking around."

"I'm with you," I said. "Besides, it's almost time for dinner, and my mom will be really mad if I'm late."

"It would be kind of hard to explain to her that you were out looking for an alien," agreed Sandy. "What were all those things?"

"I guess whatever it is dresses up like a human," I said. "Those must be its masks. That's how it manages to look like just another kid."

"It gives me the creeps to even think about it," said Sandy. "I can't believe I had that, that *thing* in my house, sleeping next to me. She seemed so normal, just like any other girl." Sandy shuddered.

"We have to decide what we're going to do," I said. "As far as we know, there are only two of them—Orents and Marilyn. At least I'm assuming Orents is an alien, too. I can't believe he's human. Maybe we can find a way to get rid of them before they can do anything."

"What about whoever Marilyn was talking to on that communication device?" said Sandy. "There could be millions of them all over the world already."

"I don't think so," I said. "If there were, they'd have taken over by now. I think they're planning something. We just have to find out what it is."

"And how do we find out?" asked Sandy.

I looked at her. We both knew the answer, but neither of us wanted to think about what it meant. "We have to get back inside that house," I said. "But it will have to wait."

"What do we do about Marilyn at school tomorrow?"

"Nothing. We have to pretend we don't know anything about what's going on. If she suspects anything, we're in big trouble."

"If they really are aliens, we're in big trouble anyway," said Sandy.

I knew she was right, and it really scared me. We walked the rest of the way home in silence. It felt really odd being the only people in the world who knew what was going on. All around us people were eating dinner and watching television just as if it was any other day. But in a house in a field on the edge of town there was an alien with a human face for a mask. And for all we knew, there was probably another one living in the Brogans' house. It may have been just another day, but it was definitely far from normal.

I said goodbye to Sandy at the corner where we'd met earlier in the day, then went home. My mother was just putting supper on the table when I walked in.

"Hey, where have you been all day?"

"Um, at the library studying with Sandy," I said. I hated to lie like that, but there was nothing else

I could think of that wouldn't sound suspicious. I felt like saying, "Out trying to save the world from invaders from space," but I'd read enough books and seen enough movies to know what happens to kids who say things like that to their parents. For the first time in my life I felt like there was nothing my parents could do to help me.

"Well, go wash up," my mother said. "It's time to eat."

All during dinner I was quiet. Normally, roast chicken is my favorite, but that night everything tasted the same to me, dull and flavorless. I felt like it was my last meal before facing something really awful.

Little did I know how true that was.

When I saw Sandy on Monday morning, she looked as though she hadn't slept all night. There were dark circles under her eyes, and she kept yawning.

"Everything okay?" I asked.

"Yeah, sure," she said. "I always spend my Sunday afternoons chasing aliens around. No big deal."

"You look awful."

"I didn't really sleep," she admitted. "I kept having these dreams about being chased by Marilyn the alien. All I could see were her glowing blue eyes."

As if she'd heard us talking about her, Marilyn

walked into the room. She walked over to us, and I waited for her to turn into the shining-eyed creature we'd seen under the plastic bubble. I looked at her face, trying to find traces of the masks we'd seen. But she looked perfectly normal.

"Hey, Sandy, that sleep-over was a lot of fun," said Marilyn. "We don't really do that where I come from."

"Thanks," said Sandy. "I'm glad you could come."

"Maybe next time we'll do it at my house," Marilyn said.

I saw Sandy's face drain of all its color as she imagined having a slumber party in the creepy old house. She managed to smile halfheartedly. "That would be great," she said.

Marilyn took her seat, and I sighed. *She didn't see us,* I mouthed to Sandy, who nodded in return. We were safe. At least for the moment.

Mrs. Weir came in to make announcements. My heart beat double-time when I saw that this time she had not one but three new students following her. They were all girls, and they were all tall and blond, just like Marilyn. In fact, they could have been her sisters. Behind me, I heard Sandy groan softly.

"Class, it seems we have some more exchange students with us," Mrs. Weir said brightly. She seemed almost a little too happy. "Our school seems to be very popular with the young Norwegian people. This is Erika, Uta, and Martina."

The three girls smiled as they were introduced. "Hello," they said in unison.

I looked around the room to see if any Westview students were missing. There were two empty seats, Sharon Duckweeder's and Butch Smirdley's. I glanced over my shoulder at Sandy, and saw that she had been doing the same thing. Suddenly, I had a very frightening thought.

As soon as the bell rang, Sandy and I rushed into the hallway to talk.

"There are three of them," I said. "And there are two Westview students missing. I think this exchange program is more like a kidnapping program. Every time one of them arrives, one of us disappears."

"But it's Sharon and Butch," said Sandy. "For all we know, they just skipped today. They've done that before. Besides, there are three new students in our class, so shouldn't three Westview kids be missing?"

"I guess so," I admitted. "But there's still some kind of connection. There just has to be."

The bell rang again, and we went to English class. When we entered Mr. Langley's room, we both stopped cold. There were at least a dozen new students sitting there. Some resembled Marilyn, and some resembled Orents. There were also at least a dozen Westview students missing.

Sandy and I took our seats. The exchange students around us smiled pleasantly and nodded. A girl next to me nodded. "Hello," she said. "I am Uta. It is nice to meet you."

"Um, thanks," I stammered. "Isn't there another Uta here, too? I think she was in my home room this morning."

The girl laughed. "Where I come from there are many Utas," she said.

Mr. Langley came in and began to talk about the weekend's reading assignment. But Sandy and I weren't paying attention. We were trying to have a whispered conversation.

"There are so many of them," she said.

"And look how many Westview students are missing," I whispered back. "Where are they?"

"And why doesn't anyone else seem to notice?" said Sandy. She was right. None of the teachers seemed to notice that all of their students were being replaced by Norwegian kids.

"Sandy and James, is there something you'd like to share with the class?" Mr. Langley asked suddenly.

Sandy and I looked at each other. "Um, no, Mr. Langley," I said.

"Then please be quiet," he said.

Mr. Langley went back to discussing the reading

assignment. I tried to be quiet, but I just couldn't. I leaned over and whispered to Sandy, "Did you notice that they all look the same?"

"James and Sandy," thundered Mr. Langley. "I thought I told you to stop talking. Now both of you can go to Principal Mulgrew's office and explain to him what you find so important that you have to disrupt class to discuss it."

Our faces bright red, Sandy and I left the classroom and headed down the hall to Principal Mulgrew's office.

"Sorry I got you in trouble," I said.

"It's okay," said Sandy. "I actually feel safer out here than I did in there. I thought if I had to sit for another minute surrounded by all of those, those . . ."

"Aliens," I said.

"Yeah, aliens," said Sandy. "I thought if I had to sit there another minute I'd start screaming. All I could think about were those heads in the house."

When we reached the door to Principal Mulgrew's office, we knocked softly. "Come in," said a gruff voice.

We opened the door and went in. I'd never been sent to the Principal's office before, and I knew for sure Sandy hadn't. We stood in front of Principal Mulgrew's desk and tried not to look at him.

"Sandy and James," he said. "I never expected to see you two here. Why don't you sit down?"

We seated ourselves in the two chairs facing Principal Mulgrew's desk. Neither of us said a word.

"What seems to be the problem?" he asked finally.

"Mr. Langley sent us," said Sandy. "We were sort of talking during class."

"Really," said Principal Mulgrew. He laughed kindly. "And what were you talking about?"

Sandy looked at me. I made a face. I didn't know what to say.

"The exchange students," Sandy said finally.

"The exchange students?" Principal Mulgrew sounded confused. "What about them?"

Sandy cleared her throat. "Well, there seem to be so many of them," she said. "We just thought it was kind of strange."

Principal Mulgrew leaned back in his chair. "I see," he said. "Do you think anything else seems strange?"

Sandy shrugged her shoulders. "There do seem to be a lot of Westview students disappearing," she said.

Principal Mulgrew smiled and laughed again. "Disappearing?" he said. "There are a lot of students choosing to become exchange students," he said. "I wouldn't say that they're disappearing."

Sandy started to say something else, but I interrupted her. "Could we become exchange students?" I asked. "Sandy and I?"

Principal Mulgrew smiled again. "Why yes, James, I think you two are most definitely excellent candidates for exchange students." Sandy was staring at me like I was crazy, but I kept talking.

"That would be great," I said. "What's the name of the student exchange program?"

Principal Mulgrew paused for a moment. His smile faded a little bit. "Why, it's called Student Exchange International," he said.

"Do you have any applications?" I asked.

Principal Mulgrew stared at me. He definitely didn't seem to be as pleasant as he had been a minute before. "No, James," he said. "I'm out of them right now. But if you come back tomorrow I'm sure I can get some more from the agency. Now I think it's just about time for your next class to begin. Let's try not to talk so much in class, shall we?"

Principal Mulgrew stood up and opened his door for us just as the bell for the next period started to ring. As we walked out, he put his hands on our shoulders. "Thank you both for coming by," he said. "I think we'll be talking more about this very soon."

Doors opened and kids streamed into the hall. Sandy and I joined the river of kids and were swept away from Principal Mulgrew's office.

"Why did you ask him if we could be exchange

students?" Sandy asked as soon as we were out of earshot.

"I wanted the name of the organization," I said. "I want to see what I can find out about them. Besides, something just wasn't right about Principal Mulgrew."

We were standing near the locker area. As we were talking, Melissa Irwin came by with a big piece of poster-board. She taped it to the wall. It was a sign announcing tryouts for the cheerleading team that afternoon. There were spaces at the bottom for interested students to write in their names.

Sandy and I walked down the hall toward our next class. At the corner, I started to enter Mrs. Eldridge's room when Sandy stopped me.

"Look," she said, pointing back down the hall.

I turned around to see what she was pointing at. Back near the lockers, Marilyn was standing talking to Principal Mulgrew. He was saying something to her and pointing at the cheerleading tryouts sign-up sheet.

A big smile crossed Marilyn's face. Then she reached into her pocket, took out a pen, and wrote her name on the list. Principal Mulgrew patted her on the back, and they both laughed. The sound floated down the hallway and made goosebumps run up and down my skin.

7

"Why was Principal Mulgrew talking to Marilyn?" I said out loud. Sandy and I were sitting at the table in her kitchen. We'd gone to her house after school to talk about what we were going to do next. There was a plate of cookies on the table. Sandy started to take a bite of one, then put it down again. Neither one of us really felt like eating. Not after what we'd seen in the hallway earlier in the day.

"I don't know," said Sandy. "And why was she so excited about signing up for cheerleading?"

"Did you notice how many new exchange students there were today?" I said.

Sandy nodded. "There were thirteen," she said. "And there were thirteen students absent today."

"How do you know that?"

Sandy grinned. "I went to the office and asked for a list. I told them the school nurse needed it."

"You're turning into a regular detective," I said. "Do you have the list?"

Sandy reached in her backpack and pulled out the list. She smoothed it out and put it on the table, so that we could both look at it.

"We could call all of their parents and see where they are," Sandy suggested. She got the phone book and looked up the first name on the list.

"Hi, Mr. Dennis. This is Sandy Taylor calling. I'm a friend of Erin's. Is she home?"

There was a pause while Sandy listened. Then she said, "Oh, she is? Well, I hope she has a good time. Thank you."

"Well?" I said after she hung up.

"Erin decided to become an exchange student in Norway," Sandy said. "One of the Utas is living there now."

We tried the next six names on the list. Each time the parent who answered told us the same story about their kid suddenly deciding to become an exchange student.

"Shall we call any more?" I asked.

"You'll just get the same answer," Sandy said. "What should we do now?"

I took a piece of paper out of my notebook. "I'm going to call Student Exchange International," I said. "Maybe we'll get some answers there."

I picked up the telephone and dialed directory information. "I'd like the number for Student Exchange International," I said to the operator.

The operator typed in the name I'd asked for.

After a moment he came back on. "I'm sorry, sir, there doesn't seem to be any listing for an organization by that name."

"Are you sure?" I asked.

I could hear him typing some more. "Nope," he said. "I even checked the rest of the area codes. No such organization in the entire state of Massachusetts."

"Thanks," I said, and hung up.

"Well," I said to Sandy. "There's no such place as Student Exchange International. It looks like someone doesn't want us to find out what's going on here."

"Mulgrew," said Sandy. "If he's involved, that would explain how all the students are disappearing without anyone in charge at school questioning it or wondering why Marilyn is living all by herself and not with a family."

"And if Mrs. Brogan is any example," I said, "the aliens are doing something to the parents so that they think everything is just fine."

"We still don't know what Marilyn was doing with all those masks," Sandy said. "Or what the pendants really do. Or why they are doing this at all. We need more information."

"We need to get back into that house," I said. "And we have to do it soon."

The next day at school, there were seven more kids missing and seven new exchange students. By

63

now it almost seemed like there were more exchange students than there were Westview kids. Everywhere I looked I saw another exchange student with a pendant. There were so many that Sandy and I were afraid to talk about the subject out loud, in case one of them should hear us.

Worst of all, nobody else seemed to be noticing anything odd. The other kids seemed really happy to have all the new exchange students, and nobody wondered where the old students had gone. In fact, I heard a couple of kids saying they couldn't wait to become exchange students themselves.

"This is too strange," I said to Sandy as we stood by our lockers between classes. "How can nobody notice what's going on?"

Just then Orents came around the corner. When he saw Sandy and I talking, he smiled his familiar, creepy smile. "Hi," he said. "What are you two up to?"

"Nothing," I said. "We were just getting ready to go to class."

Orents stared at me as if he were trying to figure something out. "Well, I just wanted to tell you that some of us are going to a movie tonight. If you two want to come, we'd love to have you."

I bet you would, I thought. What I said was, "Sorry, I have to finish a report."

"Me too," said Sandy.

"Too bad," Orents said. "I thought maybe I could

talk you two into becoming exchange students. I hear you're very interested in our program."

I cast a quick glance at Sandy. "It seems kind of interesting," I said. "You seem to be getting a lot of people involved."

Orents gave a little laugh. "We can never have too many," he said. "We love to share our country with people from other worlds. I mean, from other countries."

Sandy changed the subject. "Why are you all going out tonight?" she asked. "I mean, on a school night and all."

"We're celebrating," said Orents.

"Celebrating?" I said.

"Didn't you hear?" said Orents smugly. "Marilyn was elected head of the cheerleading squad."

I looked at Sandy. Things were getting stranger by the minute, and I was more confused than ever. Why would an alien want to be the head of a sixth-grade cheerleading squad? Orents waved to a group of other exchange students and disappeared down the hall. Sandy and I stayed by the lockers.

"Now what?" she said.

"Now we have to get into that house," I said. "And this is the perfect opportunity. Marilyn will be at the movies for at least two hours, which is more than enough time. We'll sneak into the house and be out of there before she gets back."

"I'll have to tell my mom I'm at the library

again," said Sandy. "She must think I'm doing the longest report in history."

"Hello, you two," said a voice behind us. We both jumped about a foot. When we turned around, we saw Principal Mulgrew looking at us. He was holding something in his hand.

"I have your exchange student applications," he said. "I just got a new batch in this morning, and you're the first two students I'm giving them to. Student Exchange International is looking for some new applicants, and I think you two would be perfect."

Sandy and I took the applications. "Um, thanks," I said.

"Yeah, thanks," said Sandy.

"I hope you'll have those completed and on my desk by tomorrow," said Principal Mulgrew.

"Gee, Mr. Mulgrew," I said. "I don't know if my parents will go for this," I said. "I mean, going to Norway and all."

Principal Mulgrew gave me that familiar creepy smile. "Oh, don't worry about that," he said. "I've already spoken to your parents. They think this is a fine idea. I don't think you'll get any arguments from them. Now you just make sure I get those right away. We wouldn't want you to miss out on such an exciting adventure."

With that he turned and walked away. I looked at the application in my hand.

Sandy leaned against the lockers. "What is this all about?"

"I don't know," I said, ripping the application in half. "But I think we just might find out tonight."

When I got home from school that afternoon, my mother was in the kitchen baking. My mother's a good cook, but she never bakes, so I was suspicious when I saw her sliding chocolate-chip cookies off a tray and onto a cooling rack.

"What's the occasion?" I asked, picking up a cookie and popping it into my mouth.

"Why, you're becoming an exchange student," she said. When she turned around, I nearly fainted. Pasted to her face was the same fake smile I'd seen on Mrs. Brogan. The aliens had gotten to my mother.

I concentrated really hard on sounding totally normal. If the aliens had done something to my mother, I didn't want to let on that I knew. I picked up another cookie and ate it. It was delicious. I found myself wanting more of them. There was something familiar about them, but I couldn't put my finger on exactly what it was.

"Have another one," said my mother, handing me a cookie. "Mrs. Brogan gave me these chips. Aren't they wonderful?"

That's why the cookies tasted familiar. They were just like the ones Mrs. Brogan had made.

"You know, Mom," I said, "I haven't exactly decided to become an exchange student. In fact, I kind of like it right here on Earth . . . I mean in Westview."

My mother gave me a little smile. It made her look weird, not at all like herself. "Now, dear," she said. "Your father and I think it would be a good experience for you. Besides, then we could take in an exchange student here. He could have your room. Wouldn't you like that?"

My mother was clearly gone. She had never called me "dear" in my life. I didn't know what the aliens had done to her, but I knew I wouldn't get away with disagreeing with her.

"Sure," I said. "I guess you're right. I'll think about it."

"Don't think too long, dear," she said. "You're scheduled to leave on Friday."

Friday. It was Tuesday already, which meant I only had two days before I was supposed to be taken away by aliens. There was no time to lose. I had to call Sandy.

"Thanks for the cookies, Mom," I said. "I have some homework to do before dinner. Then Sandy and I are going to study for a math test."

"That's nice, dear," said my mother. She went back to taking cookies out of the oven. She sure seemed to be making a lot of them.

I ran upstairs and picked up the phone. When Sandy answered, I told her all about my mom and what had happened. "Are your parents acting any differently?" I asked.

"Not really," Sandy said. "You know, no weirder than parents usually are."

"Well, hopefully they haven't gotten to them then," I said. "Let's meet at six on the corner and see what we can find in Hotel Alien."

After I hung up, I lay down for a rest. For some reason, my head felt a little funny.

Dinner that night was horrible. My father was acting just like my mother was, smiling and saying how proud he was that I was going to be an exchange student. Even *he* called me "dear" twice. I just ate my spaghetti and pretended everything was normal, and that my parents hadn't both turned into alien zombie slaves.

As soon as I'd helped clear the table, I pulled on my jacket, grabbed my backpack, and went to meet Sandy. We walked the distance to Marilyn's hideout quickly. We stared at the empty windows. Neither of us wanted to go inside again.

"It looks like she's gone," I said.

"It always looks like that," said Sandy. "But you're probably right. The movie should have started a few minutes ago."

"All right," I said. "Here goes nothing."

We ran for the back door, moving along the side of the house so that no one would see us. Once more I found myself at the kitchen door. I opened it, and we went inside. Everything looked exactly the same as before. Nothing had been touched.

"Where should we look?" asked Sandy.

I thought for a minute as I groped in the backpack for my flashlight. "Well, we've been in all the rooms," I said. "That leaves the attic."

The idea of going into the attic in that creepy house scared me, but I knew there was something there we hadn't found the first time. Something important. Something that would help us solve the mystery of the aliens.

We walked through the kitchen and up the familiar stairwell. At the top, I peered into Marilyn's bedroom. Just as before, there were the masks on the shelf. Their eyeless sockets stared back at me. The bed was empty, and the strange metallic curtains were pulled back.

We left the room and continued to the very end of the hall. There was another doorway there. When I opened the door, I saw a set of steps rising up into the attic. The stairwell was very narrow, so I went first, with Sandy right behind me. The stairs went up a little way, then made a sharp turn to the left. We went up another dozen or so steps, and then we were at another door.

"This is it," said Sandy.

I put my ear to the door. I didn't hear any voices coming from inside the room, so I figured it was safe to go in. The door creaked as I turned the handle and pushed. When it opened, both Sandy and I gasped. The attic was filled with different kinds of machines. All of them were covered in blinking blue and red lights.

"It looks like some kind of control room," said Sandy.

We stepped inside and started to look around at the equipment. Some looked like radios. Others were busily humming like computers. One of them had a screen, and strange letters were running across it. I shined the flashlight around, and saw that there was a pile of paper on one of the tables. I went over and looked at it.

"Come look at this," I said to Sandy.

She came over, and I showed her what I'd found. "It's a list of kids at school," I said. A lot of the names had been crossed off already.

"Those are all the kids who have disappeared," said Sandy.

I looked at the top of the list. Written across the top was STUDENTS TO BE TRANSFERRED TO VENUS.

"So they are from Venus," I said. "They must be the same aliens I read about in my book."

We looked at each other. "They're taking kids from Earth to Venus," we said at the same time.

"But why would they do that?" asked Sandy. "What do they want us for?"

71

"Let's keep looking around," I said. "There has to be something else here that will give us a clue."

Just then we heard a noise that sounded like a door opening. I paused to listen.

Someone was coming up the attic stairs.

"We have to hide!" said Sandy.

We looked around. There were no closets or anything that we could hide in. The steps were getting closer. I looked frantically for a place to go. Finally, I spied a big trunk in the corner. I grabbed Sandy's hand and dragged her over to it. Luckily it was empty. Sandy and I climbed into it and lowered the lid just before whoever was coming up the stairs reached the door. I held the lid of the trunk open slightly so that it wouldn't lock, and so I could see what was happening.

The attic door opened, and Marilyn and Orents walked in. They were laughing.

"That movie was really stupid," said Marilyn. "I can't believe humans think watching someone blow up a building is fun."

Orents laughed. "But it made the others think that we are human, too. They don't suspect a thing. It will be so easy to take them to Venus and make them our slaves. Even their parents are helping us. How did you do that?"

"It's very simple," said Marilyn. "It's all thanks to the chocolate they put into the cookies we tell them to make. They think they are using real chocolate from Norway. Little do they know it is really a Venusian mind-control drug. A few cookies, and they believe whatever we want them to." She walked over to one of the machines. "All we have to do is program thoughts into this and send the signals out. The chemical receptors in the drug pick up on the thoughts and anyone who has eaten the cookies does as we tell them."

"Brilliant," said Orents. "But why not just give all the humans this drug?"

"Because we don't want it to happen too quickly," said Marilyn. "That is the mistake we made the last time we came to this planet. We took the whole town at once and left one child behind. People took notice of our actions. This time we do not want there to be any warning signs."

Marilyn went over to one of the machines and turned it on. Letters began to flow across it, filling up the screen.

"This is our greatest plan yet," she said to Orents. He walked over to the machine and looked at what was written there. "This Saturday is the big football game at Westview Elementary. Everyone in town will be there. Naturally, the cheerleading team will perform."

"And what will happen?" asked Orents.

"The night of the game we will have a bake sale," said Marilyn. "We will sell our special cookies. Everyone will buy them and eat them. Then, during the game, I will lead the team in a special cheer. The cheer will signal our mother ship to come. At that time, the remaining humans will be taken. We will activate the mind-control drugs and they will do as we say. No one will suspect a thing."

Orents grinned. "They will all be ours," he said. "We will have more humans than we ever imagined." He started to rub his neck. "This mask is very uncomfortable," he said. "I think it is time to take it off." The next thing I knew, he was holding his face in his hands. At least, he was holding his Orents face. Instead of a human head, he had the head of a giant lizard. It was all covered in shiny blue scales.

I had to put my hand over Sandy's mouth to keep her from screaming. The Orents lizard was horrible to look at. I felt like screaming too, but I knew we'd be dead if I did.

Marilyn pulled off her head as well. "That's much better," she said. "Humans are so ugly. I hate to see myself in this thing."

The two of them remained in the room for another few minutes, looking at charts and diagrams.

Then they left, closing the attic door tightly behind them. When I was sure they were gone, I pushed open the trunk lid and stood up.

"What are they?" said Sandy in a whisper.

I climbed out of the box. "They're lizards," I said. "Lizards from Venus. And they're here to kidnap humans to use as slaves or for experiments or something. It's just like my book said. It's happening all over again, just like it did in 1933. And that stuff about the cookies. That explains why we felt funny after eating them. We must have eaten just enough to feel the drug start to work, but not enough to make us senseless."

"If they're controlling our parents' brains, how will we ever stop them?" said Sandy.

"I think I have an idea," I said. "But first we need to get out of here."

"We can't just go down the stairs and out the back door," Sandy said. "They're sure to see us."

We started to look around the attic for some way out. Besides the door going downstairs, the only other way out was through a window at one end of the room. It was painted shut, but with a lot of pushing from me and Sandy, it finally opened.

"That's a long way down," said Sandy, leaning out of the window.

I went to another trunk and opened it. Inside there were piles of old sheets. I pulled out a dozen or so and started to tie them together. Sandy saw what I was doing and started to help. Soon, we had one long rope made out of sheets.

"Now we tie it to something and climb down," I said. I found a solid beam in the attic roof and tied one end around it. I dropped the other end out of the window, where it hung down the side of the house.

"You go first," I said to Sandy. "That way I can hold this end and make sure nothing happens."

Sandy climbed onto the windowsill.

"Don't look down," I said. "Just hang on to the sheets and lower yourself down."

Sandy grabbed the rope tightly and slowly lowered herself out of the window. Going hand over hand, she inched her way down the side of the house. I hoped that Marilyn wouldn't look out the window and see her.

Sandy was a few feet from the bottom, and it looked like everything would be fine. Suddenly I felt the rope pull, and heard the sound of sheets tearing. Looking up, I saw the sheet wrapped around the ceiling beam rip. Before I could grab it, the rope slipped through my hands and over the edge of the windowsill. I heard a heavy thump as Sandy fell to the ground. I looked out to see if she was okay. She was lying on the ground, but she soon got up and dusted herself off. She waved to let me know she was all right.

I motioned for Sandy to go hide in the trees while

I thought about what to do next. Now the problem was how *I* was going to get out of the house. There were no more sheets in the trunk, and nothing else I could use as a ladder. I couldn't jump to the ground without breaking my leg, or probably both of them, and there was no way to climb onto the roof.

The only way out was for me to go through the house. That meant possibly running into Marilyn. I looked at the door leading downstairs and wished more than anything that I was home safe in my own bed. *Although even your own bed isn't safe anymore,* I thought to myself.

I opened the attic door and listened for any sounds from below. I didn't hear any, so I went down quickly. Now I was just outside Marilyn's bedroom. Standing to one side of the doorway, I peeked inside. The curtains of the bed were pulled closed, and I saw blue lights flashing on one of the machines, so I guessed she was asleep.

I was creeping past her room and heading for the stairs when suddenly I had a thought. Doubling back, I made a quick trip into the bedroom. I got what I wanted. Then I made my way down the front stairs to the first floor. I hurried through the living room and kitchen and went for the back door. I was just opening it to leave when I heard the crash of many pots and pans falling to the floor. Someone had set a trap, and I'd fallen right into it.

I grabbed the door handle and twisted it as hard as I could. Nothing happened. The door had been locked tight. I started to panic as I tried as hard as I could to get the door open. Above me, I heard the sound of feet on the floor as Marilyn woke up and left the bedroom.

I could hardly think as I looked around for a way out of the house. Marilyn was coming down the stairs, and I could hear her hissing as she slithered her way through the dark. The door was still stuck, and nothing would open it. I banged and banged on it, but it wouldn't open.

Turning around, I saw two shiny points of blue hovering in the darkness of the living room. They were Marilyn's eyes—her real, lizard ones—coming for me. I felt a scream rising in my throat as I pressed my back against the door and waited to feel her lizard claws on my neck.

The two little blue moons slid through the darkness toward the kitchen. Apparently, Marilyn couldn't see very well in the dark, because she didn't pounce on me right away. But she was moving quickly, and just the sound of her raspy hissing made my skin crawl as I waited in the dark to die.

All of a sudden, the door gave way behind me, and I felt myself falling backwards onto the porch. Marilyn heard the noise and lunged at me. I felt her fingers, or whatever she had, grab hold of my jacket. I felt her breath against my skin.

Then something else pulled me from behind, and suddenly I was free from Marilyn's grip. "Come on," I heard Sandy's voice in my ear. "Run!"

I turned and ran, not knowing where I was going or what was happening. I ran into the trees and through the field. I ran onto the road. I ran and ran until I fell down, exhausted. My lungs hurt so badly I thought I'd pass out. I'd never run so fast in my life. All I could do was lie on the ground trying to breathe.

"Are we safe?" I said, my voice coming in ragged gasps.

"For now," said Sandy. "But that was close." She was bent over, her hands on her knees, as she tried to breathe.

"You're telling me," I said. "She had me in her claws. I was almost lizard food. How'd you know where I was?"

"I heard the crash," said Sandy. "Luckily, I was able to pull the door open."

"I'm glad you did," I said.

"I don't think she followed us," Sandy said. "I wonder why?"

"Maybe she can't go outside," I said. "Maybe there's something different about our atmosphere that makes it hard for her to breathe. I'm just glad we're out of there."

"You don't think she knows it was us?" said Sandy.

"I don't think so," I said. "She probably saw our footprints in the dust on the floor from the other night and was just waiting for someone to try and come back."

"Well, now we know what they're up to," said Sandy. "I almost wish we didn't."

I fished around in my jacket pocket. "We also have this," I said. I showed Sandy what I'd taken from Marilyn's bedroom. It was one of her masks.

"What are you going to do with that?" asked Sandy.

"I'm not sure yet," I said. "I just thought it might come in useful. Right now, let's just get home."

On Wednesday morning Westview Elementary School was filled with Norwegian exchange students. Although now Sandy and I knew they were really aliens from Venus. Everywhere we looked there were new faces walking in the halls, playing in the playground, or sitting in the cafeteria. And there were more Westview students missing. Plus, all over the school members of the cheerleading squad were hanging up posters announcing Saturday's big opening game of the junior league football season.

"Everyone in town is going to be at that game," said Sandy.

"That's what they're counting on," I said. "This way they get the whole town at once and no one is left to tell about it."

"Just like Samuelstown," said Sandy.

"Except that time little Ella Crowe escaped," I said. "That's what they don't want to happen this time."

"I wonder what ever happened to her," said Sandy. "It sure would be nice to talk to her about this."

We looked at each other.

"Are you thinking what I'm thinking?" I said.

"Maybe," Sandy said. "But how do we find her?"

I thought hard for a minute. Then it came to me. "The author of the book!" I said. "We can try to call him." I pulled the book out of my backpack. I'd been carrying it around ever since we'd figured out what was going on. I looked at the information about the author on the book jacket.

"It says in the book that he lives in Boston. We can call information and ask for him."

"Do you think he'll talk to us?" asked Sandy.

"It's our only chance," I said.

Even though it was still the middle of the day, we decided to leave school and go to Sandy's house. I wasn't sure if my mother would be home or not, and I didn't want her hearing what we were doing. We walked down to the back doors of the school. We were passing the gym, and were almost at the doors, when Principal Mulgrew came around the corner. We ran smack into him.

"Well, hello there," he said cheerfully. "If it isn't the newest exchange student. How are you, James?"

"Um, I'm fine," I said. "I'm *really* looking forward to Friday."

Principal Mulgrew smiled. "Oh, so am I, James, so am I. I think you're really going to like what's in store for you." Mulgrew looked at Sandy. "As for you, young lady, I hear there are going to be some more openings soon. Perhaps you'll be joining your friend here on the adventure of your lives."

"I think I already have," said Sandy.

An odd look crossed over Principal Mulgrew's face. Then his smile returned. "Well, I'm sure you have a lot to do to get ready for your trip," he said.

"Sure," I said. "A lot. We'll see you later, Mr. Mulgrew."

As soon as Mulgrew disappeared around the corner, Sandy and I pushed open the door and left the school. As we passed the soccer field, we could see the cheerleading team practicing their new routine for the big game.

"They have no idea," said Sandy as the girls jumped up and down, waving their pom-poms. Marilyn stood at the front of the team, jumping up and down with the others and shouting cheers. I thought about the lizard beneath the mask, and wondered what the other cheerleaders would think if they could see her blue skin and shiny eyes as she belted out, "Go Westview!".

We ducked behind the parked school buses and quickly made our way to the main street of town. From there we cut down side streets until we came to Sandy's house. She went in first, to make sure no one was home. After a few minutes, she came to the door and waved me in. "Come on," she said. "They're gone."

Sandy got the phone and called information.

"I'm trying to find a number for a Michael Ford in Boston," she said.

I paused expectantly, waiting to hear what would happen next. I hoped the operator would have Mr. Ford's phone number.

"You do," said Sandy. She gave me a thumbs-up sign. "Great. I'll write it down." She scribbled a phone number on a piece of paper. Then she hung up.

"Here it is," she said proudly, waving the number at me. "You'd better call him, though. You know more about what's going on than I do."

I looked at the number. For some reason, I was very, very scared. I had no idea what I was going to say to Mr. Ford, if he even answered. He was probably going to think I was some kind of lunatic who read his book and decided to prank-call him. Worst of all, I knew that if he didn't help us, there was probably nothing I could do to stop the aliens from taking over the town.

"Here goes," I said to Sandy as I picked up the phone. There was a strange kind of buzzing on the line. "What's that noise?" I asked her. "It sounds like a bee or something."

"I don't know," she said. "It's been doing that for the past few days."

Then, as quickly as it had come, the noise went away and the line was clear again. I punched in the number. The phone rang once. Then again. Nobody picked up. I let it ring twelve times, and was just putting it down when someone picked up on the thirteenth ring.

"Hello?" The voice on the other end was gruff, and I almost hung up again.

"Hello," I said finally. "Is Mr. Ford there please?"

"Who is this?" asked the man. He sounded suspicious.

"My name is James Garcia," I said. "I read his book, *Visitors from the Skies,* and I need to talk to him."

"I'm glad you liked it," said the voice. "Now I have a lot of work to do. Goodbye."

"Wait!" I practically yelled into the phone. "Please don't hang up, Mr. Ford. I need your help."

There was silence on the other end. For a minute I thought that Mr. Ford had hung up on me. Then I heard a sigh.

"What is it?" he said. He sounded tired and irritated. "Have you seen bright lights? Is your dog acting funny? Do you think there's a ghost in your cellar? Why can't you people leave me alone."

"No," I said. "It's nothing like that." I didn't know

86

how to tell him what was happening. "It's, um, aliens."

"Aliens," he said.

"Yes," I said finally. "My school is being overrun by aliens. They're lizards from Venus, or something like that anyway. They have blue skin and shiny eyes."

"Young man," said Mr. Ford. "I'm pleased that you've read my book so carefully, and that you took the trouble to call me. But just because your teacher gave you too much homework does not mean that he is an alien."

He didn't believe me, either. I felt like crying. "Look," I said. "Kids from my school are disappearing. There's a thing with blue skin living in an abandoned house. Our parents are acting weird, and unless someone does something pretty soon all of Westview will be gone."

"Wait a minute," he said. "You say you live in Westview?"

"Yes," I said. "Why?"

There was some rustling on the other end, as if Mr. Ford were looking through a bunch of papers. Then he came back on the line. "Just as I thought," he said.

"What's wrong?" I asked. He sounded excited now.

"When Samuelstown disappeared in 1933, the

87

government ordered it removed from all the maps," he said.

"I remember that from the book," I said. "I thought it was strange that they were able to make a whole town disappear."

"Well, they didn't exactly make it disappear," he said. "I didn't put this in my book because I didn't want a bunch of people running around the new town."

"What new town?" I asked.

"Samuelstown," he said. "Or what used to be Samuelstown, anyway. See, the government didn't get rid of Samuelstown, they just renamed it. That way no one would be able to try and find evidence of the alien landing. All of the new maps simply had a different name on them."

"And what was the new name?" I asked.

"Westview," said Mr. Ford. "They renamed the town Westview. Your town is actually Samuelstown."

I felt like I'd been hit in the stomach by a baseball. I couldn't speak. All along I'd been living in the same town where Ella Crowe escaped from an alien invasion in 1933, and I didn't even know it.

"How can that be?" I asked. "How could they just create a new town?"

Mr. Ford laughed. "Oh, the government does all kinds of things most people never know about. Making new towns is just one of them. In the case of Westview, they moved in people from other parts of the country. The new townspeople never suspected that anything strange had gone on there. They thought they were just getting nice, cheap houses. Since Westview is a pretty small town, no one really noticed. Some of the old people did, but people just said they were crazy. When they died, there was no one left who even remembered Samuelstown."

I told Mr. Ford everything I knew about what was happening in Westview now, including the parts about the list of names and the way people were acting strangely.

"That all matches what Ella Crowe said," he told me when I was finished. "If I didn't believe you before, I do now. Although she never said the aliens were lizards. But I'm not sure she ever saw one without its mask. Or maybe she did and just couldn't talk about it."

"I don't blame her for that," I said. "It's nothing anyone should ever see. But why are the aliens coming back? What do they want?"

"I don't know what they want," he said. "Never really did. My guess is they've come back for more specimens to study."

"They said something about needing slaves," I told him.

"That's funny," he said. "Ella mentioned something about that when I first interviewed her. But she couldn't talk about it. Or wouldn't. I think it scared her too much."

"I thought Ella was being hidden by the government," I said.

"She was," said Mr. Ford. "But when she was in her late sixties, they let her out. I think they thought that nobody would listen to the ramblings of an old woman. And that's exactly what happened. She tried to tell people what had happened to her, and everyone thought she was just crazy. That's how I found her. I came across her file hidden with the others. But I couldn't find her anywhere. Then I read a short newspaper story about an old woman who claimed to have been the sole survivor of an alien invasion. It was in one of those newspapers they sell in grocery stores, the kind everyone thinks is made up. It was almost word for word what was in Ella's file. So I went to visit her. She didn't want to talk to me at first—thought I was just another reporter who wanted to make fun of her. But eventually she opened up, and told me the story you read in the book."

"Is she still alive?" I asked.

"Last time I checked she was," he answered. "But that was a few years ago now. She's living in an old folks' home near you, actually. I don't contact her because I don't want the government to get suspicious. They watch everything I do since I wrote that book."

"Can you tell me where she is?" I asked. "Maybe she can help us."

There was silence as Mr. Ford thought about my request. "Okay," he said. "I'll tell you, but only because I believe your story."

Mr. Ford gave me the address, and I wrote it down on a piece of paper.

"Thanks a lot," I said. "I know there's got to be a way to stop these aliens."

"I hope so," he said. "If you don't, we'll all be in trouble."

I said good-bye and started to hang up. But Mr. Ford stopped me.

"Wait," he said. "There's one more thing you should know. Something that might help you defeat the aliens."

"What is it?"

Before he could tell me, I heard the sound of breaking wood on the other end of the phone, as though a door were being smashed open. Then I heard scuffling sounds.

"What's going on?" I said.

I heard Mr. Ford shouting. "No!" he screamed. "Get away from me. Help!"

"Mr. Ford!" I yelled. "What's going on?"

There were more scuffling sounds, and the sound of glass breaking. I heard more yelling, and then nothing.

"Mr. Ford!" I yelled. "Mr. Ford?"

Someone picked up the phone. I heard the eerie sound of someone—or more likely something—hissing into the receiver. Then the line went dead.

"They must have gotten him," I said to Sandy. "The aliens must have found him."

"But how?" she said. "How would they know we were talking to him?"

I remembered the faint buzzing I'd heard when I picked up the phone. "They must have bugged the phone," I said. "It's the only way. They traced the call and found him."

Sandy's face was white as a sheet. "It's been buzzing like that for a few days now," she said. "Then they definitely know about us. Now we're really in trouble."

"We just have to stay out of sight," I said. "That means not going back to school until we've figured out a way to get rid of the aliens."

"What about our parents?" she said. "If the aliens know about us, then won't they come after our families? We can't hide from them."

"They've already gotten to mine, remember. And they're going to try and get rid of me on Friday. I don't think they've done anything to your folks yet, so you're probably okay for now."

"What did Mr. Ford tell you?" Sandy asked.

I repeated our conversation word for word, telling Sandy all about how Westview was really Samuelstown.

"That's really creepy," she said. "You mean we're all living in houses where the people were kidnapped by aliens?"

"It looks that way," I said. "And it seems it's all happening again, too."

"Did he say how to stop them?"

"He tried to," I said. "That's when I heard all those noises and the line went dead."

"Every time we seem to be getting somewhere, they interfere" said Sandy. "There's no way we can stop these things."

"We still have one clue," I said. I held up the piece of paper in my hand. "We still have Ella Crowe."

"Ella Crowe is over seventy years old and lives in a home," said Sandy. "How is she going to help? And how will we even get in to see her?"

"This address is in Cranston," I said. "That's only an hour or so from here. We can take the bus."

"You know we aren't allowed on the bus by ourselves," said Sandy seriously.

"Oh, yeah, like saving Earth from Venusian lizards isn't a good reason to break a few rules," I said.

Sandy almost laughed at that. "I guess you're right," she said. "This all just seems like a Steven Spielberg movie or something. I can't quite believe it's really happening."

"It's happening all right, and those lizards are nothing like E.T.," I said.

"How will we get in?" said Sandy. "They're not just going to let us walk in and see her."

"We'll worry about that when we get there," I

said. "We'll have to skip school tomorrow. We'll take the bus to Cranston first thing in the morning. The important thing is that we get to her before the Venusians do. Otherwise it's all over."

The front door opened and Sandy's mother came in. We heard her calling hello as she walked in.

"You'd better go," said Sandy. "We don't want her to get suspicious."

"Right," I said. "I'll go out the back door. Meet me tomorrow morning at eight o'clock at the bus stop." I pulled on my jacket and opened the door. "And be careful," I said as I left.

That night I had a nightmare. I was running down the street of an empty town. I was banging on doors, looking for anyone who might be left. But there was nobody there. Finally I ended up in the park in the center of town. I looked up at the sky, calling out for anyone to answer me. All of a sudden I saw a ship hover over my head. It was silver, and twinkled with blue and white lights. Somehow I knew that my parents and everyone I knew was on board. It took off into the black night sky, leaving me shaking my fist and screaming.

I woke up sweating. My T-shirt was soaked, and I was shivering with cold. I looked at the clock, and it said 5:30. I was afraid to go back to sleep. I picked up a book and read until the sun came up. I had to make my parents think I was really going to school, so I showered and dressed and went down to breakfast like I did every other morning. My mother was making pancakes. I sat down, and she put a big plate of them in front of me.

"They smell delicious," I said, trying to sound cheerful.

"I made them with chocolate chips," she said.

My stomach sank. I couldn't eat the pancakes or I'd become drugged like she was. I had to find a way to get rid of them. I looked around. Jake was sitting next to me, begging for food like he usually did.

"Sorry, buddy," I said as I fed him the pancakes under the table. I hoped the mind-control drugs wouldn't work on Jake the way they worked on humans.

My mother turned around. "Well, you sure ate those quickly," she said. "Would you like some more, dear?"

I shook my head. "I have to get to school," I said. "I don't want to miss the bus again."

My mother beamed at me. "You're going to be such a good exchange student," she said.

I put on my jacket, took the brown paper lunch bag my mother handed to me, and left. As soon as I was halfway down the street, I dropped the bag into a garbage can. I didn't know what was inside, but I was pretty sure there were some chocolate-chip cookies.

A few minutes later, I was standing at the bus

stop. But Sandy was nowhere to be seen. According to the schedule, the bus would arrive in five minutes. If she wasn't there, we'd miss it and have to wait another two hours. I looked up and down the street, but there was no sign of her.

Another two minutes ticked by as I stood watching the hands on my watch turn. I really hoped that nothing had happened to Sandy. After what had happened to Mr. Ford, I was afraid for all of our lives.

I saw the bus turn the corner and drive down the street towards the stop. I didn't know what to do. I didn't want to leave Sandy behind, especially when I didn't know what had happened to her. But I also knew that it was crucial that I find Ella Crowe.

Just as the bus was nearing the stop, Sandy came running down the street. Her face was all flushed, and it looked like she'd been running for a long time.

"Sorry," she said as she reached me. "My father decided it would be nice to drive me to school today, so I had to go with him and pretend to go in. Then when he left I had to run here. I was afraid someone would see me, like Mulgrew."

"He didn't, did he?"

"I don't think he did," she said. "I was more worried about getting here."

"That's okay," I said. "You're just in time."

The bus came to a stop and the doors opened. We started to board, but the driver stopped us. "What are you kids doing out of school?" he said. "It's not a holiday or something is it?"

I looked at Sandy. I hadn't counted on anyone asking us why we were on the bus, and I didn't have an answer for the driver, who was glaring at me.

Sandy smiled at him, using the kind of smile that always makes grown-ups like her. "Today is parent-teacher conferences," she said. "We have the day off, so we're going to visit our grandmother."

The driver grinned. "Isn't that sweet," he said. "What good kids you are." He let us on and shut the doors, and the bus pulled onto the street.

"Visiting our grandmother?" I said as we found our seats and sat down. "How'd you come up with that one?"

"Well, we are visiting an old person," she said. "And I thought it might come in handy when we get to the home. I was just kind of practicing."

"Well, I'm glad it worked," I said. "I don't know what we would have done if it hadn't."

We sat and looked out the window as the town slipped away and turned into wide open country-side. Soon we were riding on a long road sur-rounded by trees.

"This seems like it's the middle of nowhere," said

Sandy. "Why would anyone build a home for old folks out here?"

"Maybe they don't want anyone visiting," I said. I had no idea what kind of home Ella lived in, but it *was* pretty far away from everything.

When the bus stopped at Cranston, Sandy and I got off. There wasn't much there, just a few old houses and some rusting cars that looked like they hadn't been driven in a long time. A dirt road stretched off in one direction, and the highway went in the other.

"This looks like a ghost town," Sandy said. "What's the place we're looking for?"

"It's called Shady Elm Home," I said, looking around at the deserted town. "I bet they don't get many visitors."

Since the dirt road seemed the only way in or out of town besides the highway, we started to walk down it. After a few minutes we arrived at a huge iron gate. Behind it sat an enormous old house. It looked more like a castle than a house, with high stone towers and narrow little windows in the walls. A tall iron fence ran around the whole thing.

A man came out from a little guard booth and walked over to the gate. "Can I help you?" he asked. He wasn't smiling.

"We're here to see our grandmother," I said. It had fooled the bus driver, and I hoped it would fool the guard.

The guard frowned. "What's her name?"

"Ella," I said. "Ella Crowe."

The guard grunted. He looked at a list attached to a clipboard, and then back at us. "Go in," he said.

He pushed a button, and the big iron gates swung open. We walked through and started up the long driveway. "That was close," I said.

We came to the house and went up the steps. Inside, the place looked almost like a hotel. A woman was sitting behind a desk, and I went over to her.

"We're here to see our grandmother," I said. "Ella Crowe."

The woman looked at me. She looked like she was thinking about something. Then she smiled. "Certainly," she said. "Just one moment." She picked up a telephone and punched in some numbers. After speaking briefly with someone, she hung up.

"Ella's in the garden," she said. "You will find her through that door."

Sandy and I went through the door the woman had pointed to and into a big garden. We looked around, and under one of the large trees we saw an old woman. She was sitting on a bench and looking at the sky.

"That must be her," I said.

Sandy and I walked over and approached the woman. As we came nearer, she didn't take any notice of us. She just kept looking up at the clouds as though she were waiting for someone.

"Hello, Ella," I said.

The woman didn't look at me. She was small, and her skin was very wrinkled. Her dark eyes were very bright, and her hair was pure white. She was wearing a green wool coat. I said "hello" again, but she didn't seem to hear me.

Sandy tried. "Hello, Ella," she said. "How are you?"

Ella blinked. "They're coming back, you know," she said. Her voice was small and soft, like a little girl's. Still she didn't stop staring upward.

"Who is?" I said. "Who's coming back, Ella?"

"The blue eyes," she said. For the first time, she turned and looked at me. "The blue eyes are coming back. And this time no one can stop them."

"We need your help," I said to Ella. "People are disappearing."

"Kids are disappearing," added Sandy.

"Mr. Ford is missing," I said.

Ella laughed, a high, giggly laugh. She covered her mouth with her hands. "I told him they would come," she said. "I told him not to talk." She went back to staring at the sky.

I didn't know what to say next. Ella did kind of seem crazy. Maybe everyone was right, maybe she had made it all up. Maybe Sandy and I were crazy, too. Nothing made any sense.

"What can we do?" I said to Ella, hoping she'd answer me. She didn't. She started humming "Ring Around the Rosie" to herself.

Sandy was looking around the garden. "Who's that?" she said, pointing.

I turned around. Walking across the grass were two men. They looked like security guards. They seemed to be moving quickly.

"I don't know," I said. "But I don't like the looks of them."

When the men saw us looking at them, they began running toward us.

"I think we'd better leave," I said to Sandy.

I started to move, but felt something gripping my wrist. It was Ella. Her bony fingers circled my arm and clutched me tightly. She was looking right into my eyes, and this time there was nothing crazy about her at all. "The pendants," she said.

I looked over my shoulder. The men were getting closer. "What about the pendants?" I asked.

"The pendants allow them to speak and breathe," she said. Then she let go and started laughing, loudly and crazily, as I ran for my life.

The men were only yards from us. Sandy and I ran as fast as we could away from them. The ground was slippery with fallen leaves, and several times I lost my balance and almost fell on my face. The men were gaining on us.

"It was a trap," said Sandy as we ran. "They knew who we were when we walked in."

"But how?" I said. "How could they possibly know."

We ran around the corner of the big house and found ourselves trapped by the iron fence that ran around the property. It was too tall for us to climb over, but there was a small gate. I rattled the bars, but the latch was rusted shut and refused to open. The security guards turned the corner and started coming towards us. There was nowhere for us to go. The guards were grinning wickedly.

"This is it," Sandy said. "We're finished."

I gave the gate another shake, throwing my

shoulder against it as hard as I could. All of a sudden, there was the sound of metal scraping against metal and the rusty latch gave way. The gate swung open just wide enough for Sandy and I to squeeze through.

We ran as fast as we could down the driveway toward the big front gate. Behind us, the men were trying to push the gate open wide enough for them to follow us, but it was stuck fast. I just hoped it would stay that way. Then, as the front gate guard saw us approaching, he began to shut the gates. They were quickly closing together, the gap between them narrowing.

Sandy and I made one final dash for the disappearing opening. We slipped through the gates just as the gap was closing and ran as fast as we could away from the house. We made it into town in record time. The bus returning to Westview was coming down the road just as we arrived. We looked behind us, but it seemed no one had followed us.

Luckily, we didn't have the same bus driver that we'd had coming to Cranston. This one didn't give us any trouble as we got on and found our seats.

"That was really close," I said as I leaned back and shut my eyes.

"It sure was," said Sandy. "I thought for sure those guys were going to get us. The guard at the gate must have told them who we were there to see. What did Ella tell you?"

I told Sandy what Ella had said about the pendants allowing the aliens to speak English and to breathe.

"That explains why they never take them off," said Sandy. "And why Marilyn didn't chase us. They probably can't breathe our air. And the pendants must act as translators of some kind, so that the alien language comes out as English."

"I don't know how that's going to help, though," I said. "We can't steal all of their pendants."

Sandy looked thoughtful. "We can't get *all* of them," she said. "But maybe we can get *one* of them."

"What do you mean?" I said. "How's that going to help?"

Sandy smiled. "I have an idea," she said.

By the time the bus pulled into Westview, Sandy had outlined her plan to me. If it worked, we'd be able to stop the aliens before the mother ship arrived.

We said goodbye, and headed off to our homes. My mother didn't even seem to notice that I was late. She was busy making a meatloaf when I walked in, and the only thing she seemed concerned with was whether or not she'd put enough bread crumbs in with the hamburger.

"Hello, dear," she said. "How was school?"

"Just fine," I said, running out before she could ask anymore questions.

That night after dinner my mother insisted on helping me pack a suitcase for my trip the next day. I sat on my bed watching as she folded up my clothes and put them into the bag. I wondered where she really thought I was going.

"The people from SEI will be here at seven o'clock to pick you up," she said. "They said it would be better for you to take a night flight so that you can sleep on the plane and not be too tired when you arrive in Norway."

"I'll bet they did," I muttered. I wondered who exactly these people were, and where they took the kids after they picked them up. I suspected they brought them to the house Marilyn was staying in and then had a spaceship pick them up late at night when it brought the other alien exchange students. That would explain the blue lights people had been seeing. Whatever they did, one thing was for sure: I didn't want to find out firsthand.

"Of course, I packed a whole box of cookies for you to take on the flight," my mother said. She held up a cardboard box for me to see before placing it in the bag.

When she'd finished packing, she gave me a kiss and left. I lay in my bed, thinking about the aliens. I couldn't let them take me, that was for sure, even if I was curious about where they went.

As I tried to go to sleep, a lot of things went through my mind. I wondered how many other towns across the country were experiencing the same thing Westview was, and if somewhere there was another kid lying in her bed trying to figure out what to do about all the exchange students suddenly showing up at her school. I thought about Ella, and how she was being held captive in Shady Elm. I thought about what might happen if our plan didn't work.

Eventually, I fell asleep. This time I dreamed that I was actually *on* one of the alien ships. I was tied to a table, and there were aliens standing around me. They were all holding sharp instruments. They were talking about me.

"We need to alter his brain," one of them said. "Otherwise he won't make a good slave." The alien moved toward me with the instrument in its hand. I started to scream.

That's when I woke up. It was morning, and my father was knocking on the door. He opened it and looked in.

"Time to get up, buddy," he said. "It's your last day in Westview for a while." He gave me a big fake smile and then left.

It's my last day on Earth, I thought. What I said was, "Okay, Dad, I'll be right down."

I sat through yet another cheerful breakfast, pretending to be happy while my mother chattered about what a fun time I'd have in Norway.

"You can learn to ski," she said. "I hear they have a lot of snow there."

"Great," I said. "That will be fun."

I finished my food as quickly as I could and got up to go.

"Don't be late coming home," my mother said as I left for school. "You don't want to keep the SEI people waiting."

"Don't worry," I said. "I'll be here."

As I walked into school, the first person I ran into was Principal Mulgrew. When he saw me, he grinned. "Guess we won't be seeing you for a while after today," he said, patting me on the shoulder.

"Guess not," I said. By now I was sure he was in on the whole thing with the aliens, and I didn't want to be anywhere near him.

"I don't know what your little friend will do without you," he continued. "You two seem to do a lot together." From the way he said it, I wondered if he knew what we had done the day before.

"She'll be okay," I said. He was making me really uncomfortable, and I wanted to get away. "I have to get to class now."

I ran down the hall to homeroom. By now all but a handful of kids were exchange students. I didn't have time to notice who else was missing as I sat down. I did notice that Orents was staring at me.

"Hi," I said to Sandy.

"Hi," she said back. "You all set for your trip?"

"All packed," I said.

On the bus home from Cranston we'd planned the conversation. I wanted Orents, and anyone else who might be suspicious, to think I was ready to become an exchange student. I saw him smile when he heard me, and I winked at Sandy. The plan was working perfectly. Now if only the rest of it went as smoothly, we'd be okay.

The school day went by very quickly. Because Sandy had band practice, we didn't see each other at lunch. I spent the time watching Marilyn and her cheerleader friends put up more posters about the big game and the bake sale. As I watched her laughing and joking, I got madder and madder. I couldn't stand the idea of the aliens invading my school and taking my friends who-knew-where. Finally, I threw my sandwich away and went for a walk.

As I passed by the art room, I happened to notice a bunch of heads sitting on a table. They weren't the kind of heads we'd seen in Marilyn's house— they were made out of newspaper and paste. People had painted them to look like real people. As I looked at them, it gave me an idea. I made sure no one was looking, then I grabbed one of the heads and stuck it in my backpack.

After school, Sandy and I walked home together. As we did, I told her my plan.

"That's great," she said when I'd finished.

"And then I'll come and get you," I said. "And we can put the rest of your plan into action."

"This is a piece of cake," Sandy said. "We'll get rid of those aliens before they know what hit them." She high-fived me. We were as good as done with the Venusians.

I left Sandy and started to walk home. Our combined plans were really great, and for the first time since it had all started I felt confident that everything would be okay again.

Boy, was I in for a surprise.

For dinner that night my mother made my favorites—lasagna and apple pie. It was supposed to be this great going-away dinner, but it was hard to enjoy it with my parents acting so strangely and with me worried about pulling off the plan for defeating the aliens. Still, I managed to pretend everything was fine. When dinner was over, I even helped my mother do the dishes. Afterwards, I said I had some last minute packing to do.

"Just make sure you're ready by seven," my mother said.

I looked at my watch. It was twenty minutes after six. *Oh, I'll be ready,* I thought as I ran up the stairs.

Once I was in my room, I shut and locked the door. Then I opened the suitcase my mother had packed and began to pull things out of it. I put some of the clothes into my backpack. Then I took a bag out from under the bed. Inside it was some food I'd taken from the kitchen when no one was looking. I shoved that inside the backpack, too, along with my flashlight.

Then I set the first part of the plan into action. I took off the clothes I was wearing and changed into new ones. Then I took the clothes I'd been wearing all day and started to stuff them with bunched-up newspapers I'd taken from the garage. When they were filled, I set the shirt on top of the jeans and tucked the ends inside the jeans. The thing I'd made looked kind of like a scarecrow, only with no head.

I set the dummy me in my desk chair, with its back to the door so it would look like I was reading. I tucked the ends of the jeans into some old tennis shoes. Then I took the paper-and-paste head I'd taken from the art room and placed it in the neck of the shirt. The head was a little small and bumpy, but when I put my baseball cap on it, it really did look like me from the back. Anyone looking in would have to get close to realize that it wasn't me. That's what I was counting on.

Once I was sure the dummy looked real, I picked up my backpack. It was ten minutes to seven. I

111

unlocked my door, but kept it closed. Going to my window, I opened it and looked out. There was a big tree outside. When I was little, my father and I had built a treehouse in it. I'd used it a lot then, but hadn't been in it for a long time. Still, I remembered the trick of climbing from my window to the big branch outside.

I shimmied along the branch until I reached the treehouse. Climbing inside, I put down my backpack and looked around. I'd already put a sleeping bag in there, and everything looked fine. No one would ever think to look for me there. I could hide out until the next day, when it was time for Sandy and me to put part two of the plan into action.

Going back to the treehouse window, I looked into my room. I looked at my watch. It was seven o'clock. Then I heard the sound of a car or truck pulling up in front of the house. I knew it was the student exchange people. I ducked down so no one who might look out the window could see me, and waited.

A few minutes later, I saw the door to my room open. My mother's face appeared. Someone was behind her. It was Principal Mulgrew.

I knew he was in on it, I thought. *He's a traitor to all humans.* I wondered what the aliens had promised him in exchange for his help.

I watched as Principal Mulgrew said something. When what he thought was me didn't respond, he went over and touched the dummy on the shoulder. When he did, the head fell off and rolled across the floor. I could see my mother's mouth open in a scream. Then she fainted.

Principal Mulgrew was shouting and waving his hands. I saw him rushing around the room, looking for me. He even came to the window and looked out. I ducked just in time, but not before I saw something. One of his eyes was glowing—and it was bright blue.

He's not human at all, I thought. *He's one of the aliens, too.*

Suddenly it dawned on me: the aliens had been sending spies to Earth for years, disguising them as grown-ups. The alien spies became teachers and principals and other kinds of things that would put them near children. Now the aliens were coming to get all of the kids. No one stopped them because all the people in charge were aliens, too!

I peered back out the window. Principal Mulgrew had disappeared. My father was sitting on my bed, trying to wake up my mother. I wanted to tell them I was okay, that I was only a few feet from where they were, but it was too risky. I had to get to Sandy and tell her what I'd discovered. I was risking getting caught, but she had to know.

I knew Mulgrew was probably out looking for me, so I was careful to walk only in the shadows as I made my way to Sandy's house. It was dark anyway, but I still kept away from the streetlights. I didn't want to take the chance of running into Mulgrew or anyone else.

When I got to Sandy's house, I looked for any signs of an unfamiliar car or of Principal Mulgrew. Everything looked fine, so I went to the door and knocked. Sandy's father answered.

"Oh, hello, James," he said. "I didn't expect to see you here."

"Is Sandy in?" I asked.

"Well, no, she isn't," said Mr. Taylor. "Didn't you know?"

"Know what?" I said.

Mr. Taylor smiled. "Sandy's become an exchange student," he said. "She left about fifteen minutes ago."

12

I stared at Mr. Taylor in disbelief.

"An exchange student?" I said. "She didn't say anything to me about becoming an exchange student."

"We wanted to surprise her," said Mr. Taylor. "They thought it would be a good idea."

"Who thought it would be a good idea?" I asked. I was starting to get a horrible feeling in my stomach.

"The people from Student Exchange International," he said. "They said it would be best not to mention it."

That's when I saw that Mr. Taylor was eating a cookie. He held the half-eaten treat in his hand, as though I had interrupted him in the middle of chewing it. He noticed that I was looking at him.

"Would you like a cookie?" he asked. "Mrs. Brogan gave Sandy's mother the recipe. It's made from Norwegian chocolate. I can't eat enough of them."

"No, thanks," I said. "I'm allergic to chocolate. I have to go now." I felt really sick.

"I'm sorry you missed Sandy," said Mr. Taylor.

"Yeah, me too," I said. I turned and ran for home.

Only there was no home anymore. And there was no Sandy. I had nowhere to go and no one to talk to. I couldn't believe that the aliens had gotten Sandy. They must have had the whole thing planned all along. I thought back to the day when I had called Mr. Ford and heard someone listening in on the conversation. The aliens had to have known it was Sandy and me. Then they let me know I was being taken as an exchange student so that Sandy would never suspect that she was being kidnapped too.

Their plan had worked, at least partly. They had Sandy. But they didn't have me. Now I *had* to succeed in the plan Sandy and I had come up with. As I raced for my house, I tried to remember everything Sandy had thought of. It was going to take a lot of careful planning to pull off what she had in mind.

When I got to my house, I made sure the coast was clear before I climbed the fence and went up into the treehouse. I shut the trapdoor that led to the ladder. There was no way anyone could get in without me hearing them.

I opened the backpack and pulled out some food. I'd taken some crackers and peanut butter from the kitchen, as well as a Thermos of milk. I sat in the dark treehouse and ate the crackers dipped in peanut butter while I planned my attack. I'd never felt so alone. My mind kept focusing on Sandy and where she was. I remembered my dream about the aliens wanting my brain, and shuddered. I hoped she was all right.

After I ate, I tried to go to sleep. Strangely, it was very peaceful in the treehouse. I actually felt safe lying twelve feet above the ground. Before I knew it, I was asleep.

When I woke up on Saturday morning, my first thought was that I wanted to go down and have some cereal and watch cartoons. Then I remembered where I was. I stretched inside my sleeping bag. I was tired and sore from having slept on the hard wooden floor. But at least I was still alive. I hoped Sandy was.

I reviewed the plan Sandy had come up with. The big game was supposed to start at five o'clock. Everyone in town was going to be there because it was a big deal for the school. We knew that the cheerleaders were going to be selling cookies before the game—the chocolate-chip mind-control cookies that had been making everyone behave so strangely.

We also knew that Marilyn had taught the cheerleaders a special new routine to do during halftime. The routine was supposed to summon the alien mother ship, and everyone at the game would then be kidnapped. Because their minds would be controlled by the cookies, they wouldn't even put up a fight.

Sandy's plan was for her to dress up like a cheerleader and try to get onto the field. She thought that if she could interrupt the routine that the mother ship wouldn't know when to come. While she was doing that, I was supposed to try to get to Orents and destroy the mind-control device. With Sandy gone, I had to do everything myself. But I didn't know how I'd be able to stop the cheerleaders.

I opened my backpack. Inside I had stuffed the mask I'd taken from Marilyn's house. I held it up and looked at it. I knew what I would do.

Getting into the school was easy. All I had to do was slip in the door near the gym, which was always open in case members of the teams were running laps or practicing late. I checked that no one was in the hallways and then dashed for the locker room.

Once I was safely in the locker room, I opened my gym locker and shoved my backpack inside. I checked my watch. It was almost three o'clock. I knew the cheerleading team would be practicing until three-thirty. The football team would start suiting up at four. That gave me only about half an hour to do what I had to do and get out of there.

I ran through the gym to the entrance to the

girls' locker room. Checking behind me to make sure no one was there, I stuck my head inside the room. Thankfully, it was empty. I went inside.

Sandy had told me that the cheerleaders always kept their uniforms hanging in the locker room before a big game. With any luck, I'd be able to grab a uniform and get out quickly. That was the easy part.

After a minute of searching, I found the uniforms hanging on a rack near the lockers. As I was taking one, I heard voices. The cheerleaders were coming back into the locker room! I couldn't let them see me, or everything would be ruined.

I couldn't find a place to hide. There were no closets or anything. Finally I fumbled with the handles on the tall lockers until one opened. It was just big enough for me to fit into. I squeezed inside and held the door shut. I couldn't see anything, but I could hear just fine. I heard the girls talking as they came in and started dressing for the game.

"This is so cool," said one. "Marilyn, that new routine is out of this world."

In more ways than one, I thought.

"Thanks," said Marilyn. "Now let's get dressed. We have to get out there and sell cookies. The crowd should be arriving soon, and we certainly don't want to miss anyone." She sounded really happy, like she couldn't wait to take over the world.

I wanted to jump out and get her right then. But I kept quiet.

It seemed like forever while I waited for the girls to leave. Finally, they had all gotten into their uniforms and left. No one seemed to notice that a uniform was missing. I figured they must have extras, in case someone got theirs dirty.

When it was quiet, I slowly opened the locker door. I was alone. I checked my watch and saw that I only had five minutes before the football team showed up. Snatching up a pair of pom-poms that someone had left behind, I ran back to the boys' locker room and grabbed my bag out of the locker. Running outside, I made my way to the football field.

Marilyn had been right—there were lots of people arriving for the game. Parents and kids were all crowded around. And all of them were eating chocolate-chip cookies. Marilyn and her squad had set up tables all over the place, and they were selling cookies by the dozens. Everywhere I looked I saw people munching on the mind-control treats.

Slipping through the crowd, I hid beneath the bleachers at one end of the field. It was dark under there, and I knew no one would be able to see me. In the darkness, I pulled the cheerleading uniform out of my bag. Originally, the plan had been for Sandy to dress as a cheerleader and try to upset the routine. Now that she had been captured, it was up to me.

I pulled my jeans off and quickly slipped into the cheerleading costume. It was a little too small, but I got it on and zipped it shut. I couldn't believe I was wearing a blue and green skirt. But if it would save my friends, my parents, and my town, I'd do it.

As I finished dressing, I heard noises coming from one end of the bleachers. It sounded like people whispering. Creeping over towards the sound, I tried to figure out who was talking. It was Marilyn, and she was talking to Orents.

"You sit in the front row," she was saying. "This box will control the thoughts of the people who have taken the drug, which thanks to my cookies is all of them. When I complete the routine, the ship will land. You will make sure that all of the humans are under control. Then we will lead them on board and take them back to Venus."

Orents nodded. "These humans are so stupid," he said.

Marilyn laughed. "Yes, look how we tricked that fool Garcia. By letting him think he was the one we wanted, we got the girl with no trouble at all. And tonight we will get him as well."

"Do you think he's here?" asked Orents. I was pleased to see that he sounded a little worried.

"Don't worry," she said. "We will find him. And when we do, he will be the first to go."

Marilyn and Orents left, heading for the field. I was tempted to run after them and tackle them, but I knew I had to wait. One mistake and it would all be over.

I sat under the bleachers as the game began. It was strange hearing the roars of the crowd when I couldn't see what was happening on the field. As I sat there, surrounded by the screams and cheers, I tried to work up the courage for what was coming. It was me against all of the aliens. The fate of Westview, and possibly of the whole world, was in my hands.

It seemed to take forever for the first half to be over. Finally, I heard the whistle blow for halftime. Everyone applauded as Marilyn and her team came onto the field. It was time for me to go.

Emerging from under the bleachers, I snuck around until I was on the edge of the field. In my hand was the mask of Marilyn's face. I stood in the shadows, watching as she led the cheerleaders onto the field. When the last one was running by, I tripped her. She sprawled on the ground.

"Sorry," I said as I ran onto the field. "But you'll thank me later." I slipped on the mask. It didn't fit very well, and it was hard to see through the eye holes, but I could tell where I was going. I ran onto the field, waving my pom-poms. I could feel the fake hair flying around my head.

I joined the other girls on the field. I'd seen the

routine before, so I kind of knew what they were going to do. But I'd certainly never been a cheerleader. I tried to watch the girls and follow what they did. I waved my pom-poms and screamed. I kicked and twirled. Some of the girls were giving me strange looks, but they were so busy cheering they barely noticed me. Marilyn had her back to me, so she didn't know I had infiltrated her team. Or that I had her extra face on.

Everything was going pretty well. It was mainly a lot of running around. Most of the routine was just getting people to cheer along with us. The crowd was so worked up they would have cheered for anything.

"Two. Four. Six. Eight," Marilyn chanted into the megaphone she was carrying. "Who's the team that's really great?"

"Westview!" screamed the crowd. They were stamping their feet and cheering as Marilyn and the squad danced and kicked. The routine was going according to plan, and I knew the big moment was about to happen. When the girls began to form a pyramid, I knew that the routine was almost over.

I ran over to where the cheerleaders were climbing onto one another's shoulders. Two girls were hoisting Marilyn up onto the top to form the tip of the pyramid. As they lifted her off the ground, I grabbed her skirt and pulled. She came crashing down on top of me.

"What are you doing?" she screamed. "You're ruining our routine."

I pulled off my mask so that Marilyn could see who I was. "I'm saving the Earth," I said. I could hear people in the stands booing. They thought someone was ruining the show, too.

I reached down and pulled the pendant from around Marilyn's neck. As soon as I did, she started to cough. She also started to hiss, because without her translator she couldn't speak English.

All of a sudden I saw several football players and cheerleaders coming at me. All of them were wearing the same pendants.

"Stay back!" I yelled. "If you don't, I'll smash this pendant to dust and she'll die!"

The aliens backed away, but they stayed nearby, watching my every move. The people in the stands were talking. I held my arm around Marilyn's throat so that she couldn't get away. She was weakened from not being able to breathe properly, and didn't put up a fight.

"What's going on?" yelled someone in the crowd.

I grabbed the megaphone that the cheerleaders had been using to call out cheers. "Listen," I shouted to the people in the stands. "You are in danger. These exchange students are not what they seem."

Reaching behind Marilyn's neck, I found the snap that held her mask on. Undoing it, I pulled the mask from her head. When the people in the stands saw her blue lizard head, they gasped.

"She's a lizard!" shouted a woman.

"They're all lizards," I yelled. "The ones with the pendants. Grab them."

Suddenly, the people in the stands were moving, trying to get hold of anyone who was wearing a pendant. The aliens ran, trying to get away. But many of them were captured.

That was when I saw Orents. He was sitting in the front row, busily typing something into the mind-control box. I knew that any second the people in the stands would turn into mindless robots under his control. I had momentarily broken through the control of the mind drug by shocking them with Marilyn's unmasking. But soon Orents would increase the power of the box. Then they wouldn't be able to hold the lizards captive.

Dropping Marilyn, I ran as fast as I could towards Orents and dove at him. I felt my arms close around him as I fell, knocking him to the ground. I snatched the box from his hands and hurled it to the ground. It smashed into a hundred pieces.

Orents looked up at me. He was whining and crying. "Don't hurt me," he said. "Please don't hurt me."

I grabbed his pendant and snapped the chain. Then I pulled his mask off. His little lizard mouth opened and his tongue slid in and out as he gasped for breath.

"Now let's see you make a slave of Sandy," I said.

Over my shoulder, I heard the sounds of people talking. I turned around, expecting to see captured exchange students. Instead, what I saw was a spaceship. It was hovering over the field, and its blue and silver lights were twinkling.

It was the spaceship from my dreams. Only this time it was real. I was too late.

13

The spaceship was bigger than anything I'd ever seen. It looked almost like a small city, with towers and spires and windows all over it. The whole thing was twinkling with lights, and it made a weird humming sound. Everyone around the football field was staring up at the ship.

I picked up the megaphone again.

"Everyone with captive aliens, come over here," I shouted. People moved towards me, pushing and pulling alien captives with them. Some of the aliens still had on their masks. Others had been revealed as blue lizards. The aliens stood in a group, surrounded by humans. There were about fifty or so of them.

I grabbed Orents by the collar and pulled him up. "Who's in that thing?" I demanded.

Orents hissed at me. I'd forgotten that I'd taken his pendant. I handed it to him, and he held it to his throat.

"That is the mother ship," he said. "It will take

all of you to Venus, where you will be our slaves." His voice crackled and hissed. I guessed that I'd broken the translator when I grabbed it.

I shook Orents. "Tell whoever's in it to come out," I said. "I want to talk."

Orents was silent. I shook him again. "Look, you creepy lizard, I want my friends back! Now get someone down here now or I'll have these people take away all your little pendants. Do you want to see how long you'd live breathing just Earth air?"

Orents looked around nervously. I could tell he was thinking about what it had been like to breathe oxygen. Still, he didn't say anything.

"Take their pendants off," I yelled through the megaphone. "Smash them." The humans reached for the pendants.

"Wait," Orents said. He looked defeated.

"Okay," I said, handing him the megaphone. "Tell your leader I want to talk, and I want to talk now."

Orents hissed something into the megaphone. A few seconds went by, and then I heard similar hissing sounds coming from the spaceship.

"What did they say?" I asked.

"He's coming down to talk to you," said Orents.

"Who is?"

"Our leader."

"What's his name?" I demanded.

Orents hissed again. "In your language you would call him Urzel."

I watched as a small opening appeared in the bottom of the ship. A long ramp extended to the ground, and clouds of smoke billowed out from the doorway. After a minute, I saw someone walking down the ramp through the smoke.

I couldn't believe my eyes. It was a giant lizard. He was about eight feet tall, and he was covered with bright blue scales. Only instead of wearing a mask like the other lizards, he was wearing a glass helmet that covered his head. I could see his long tongue darting in and out as he looked around him. Urzel walked over to where I was standing with Orents.

"What do you want, human?" he asked.

"I want an exchange," I said. "I will return your people if you return the humans you've taken away."

Urzel hissed through his helmet. It sounded like he was laughing at me. "And if I refuse?"

I pointed to where Marilyn lay on the ground. She was still alive, but she was barely breathing. "Or I will destroy all of the pendants," I said.

Urzel smiled, as much as a giant blue lizard from Venus can smile. "I would still have my prisoners," he said. "A few lost lives would be worth having so many new slaves, don't you think?"

Orents began to cry. "I don't want to die," he said.

"I don't think you'd give up some of your best scientists just to keep a few Earth people," I said. I guessed he was bluffing and hoped I was right.

Urzel was silent for a minute, staring at me.

Then he spoke. "I will give you back your people, human," he said. "But we will be back again some-day. And next time there will be no mistakes."

He spoke into a communicator on his wrist. Another door appeared in the spaceship, and dozens of humans began to come out. They wandered onto the football field looking confused and surprised, as though they had been asleep. Some were grown-ups, but most were kids. I saw a lot of kids from school. They ran to their parents who, free from the mind-control drugs, hugged them.

I saw Sandy appear at the top of the ramp. She waved, then ran down to meet me. She stood next to me while I finished negotiating my deal with Urzel.

"Now take your people," I said when all of the humans had left the ship. "And leave."

I motioned for everyone to release the aliens they were holding. The lizards scurried for the ramp, running into the ship as quickly as they could. Two of them (one of which had been Principal Mulgrew) picked up Marilyn and carried her inside. I shoved Orents toward the ramp. He fell, then got up and ran as fast as he could through the doorway. I even saw some people I had thought were humans going into the ship, people like the local minister and the drugstore owner. It gave me the creeps thinking that all along they'd been aliens living alongside us. I was glad to see them go.

When all of the aliens were gone, Urzel turned to me. "Until next time, human," he said, and followed his people into the ship.

"We'll be ready," I said as the door shut behind him.

We all watched as the ship lit up. The football field flooded with blue light as the ship disappeared into the night sky, leaving us alone. All I heard was the sound of leaves rustling in the wind. It was a beautiful fall night, crisp and clear. Above the football field, the stars twinkled happily.

Sandy turned to me. "It's over," she said. "It's really over. You did it!"

"*We* did it," I said. "It was your plan."

"Yeah," she said. "But you're the one wearing a skirt."

I looked down. I'd forgotten that I was still dressed as a cheerleader. "Oh, great," I said. "I just saved the world and confronted a gigantic alien lizard ruler wearing a cheerleading skirt."

Sandy started to laugh. The rest of the crowd started to cheer, chanting my name. Two men picked me up and carried me on their shoulders through the crowd while people yelled, "James. James. James." As I passed through the throngs of people, I saw my parents waving to me. I waved back.

Later on, my parents and Sandy's parents took us out for pizza to celebrate. It turned out that the pizza shop owner had been a lizard, too, so we all helped make the pizzas. Sandy and I shared a pepperoni with extra cheese. Food had never tasted so good. As we ate, I told the whole story of what had happened to our parents.

"I can't believe we didn't even know what was going on," my mother said.

"I'm so sorry we let them take you," said Sandy's dad. "Those cookies really knocked us out. I had no idea what was happening."

"I actually called you 'dear'?" my mother asked.

"Just don't do it again," I said. We all laughed.

None of the people who had been captured by the aliens remembered much. They all recalled being driven to Marilyn's house and seeing a bright blue light. Then everything went black. A few said they thought they could remember lying on tables, like the one in my dream, but none of them were sure.

"I don't think I want to remember," said Sandy. "I'm just glad I'm home."

We ate pizza well into the night. Then everyone went home. Tucked into my own bed, with Jake at my feet snoring peacefully, I felt happier than I'd ever felt before. The world was safe, thanks to me and Sandy. I'd confronted the aliens and won. I fell asleep and, for the first time in three weeks, had no dreams at all.

I stared at the robot. It was ugly, and getting uglier the more attention Sandy paid to it. Another bad thing. Besides, it was off, not working, and about as entertaining to watch as the lawn mower in Dad's garage.

"Not that it matters, but what's the other brain used for?"

"Higher functions. Thinking, learning, making decisions. It's the higher brain functions that separate people from animals. When perfected, Arthur will be like us, only better. We've programmed his backup brain with incredible abilities—an encyclopedia of knowledge. He'll be able to call upon this information when needed. Virtually indestructable, he'll be able to walk through fire and survive extreme cold; he won't even need to breathe, so we can send him into space."

"Not for NASA," said Abbott, very stubbornly. Abbott had a big beef with NASA.

"Well, maybe for somebody," said Mrs. Abbott. "There will be a lot of people going to space over the next few years, and Arthur will be there."

"If he's perfected."

"He'll be perfected."

"Aye, eventually."

I was taking a closer look at this mechanical kid. "He looks like he'll be pretty strong."

"Aye, strong enough. He could lift a car over his head and balance it for a while."

"Could he throw it?"

"Why would we be wanting to throw cars around, boy?"

"Just wondered." I could imagine myself being that strong, some sort of cyborg—half-person, half-robot warrior—fighting for justice, just like in the comic books. "He could be a superhero," I said, the idea getting me excited. "Forget about sending him into space. You could program him to fight crime and search out evil. There's lots he could do. This basement could be his secret hiding place, and . . ."

I stopped talking. Half the class was staring at

me, Sandy Miller especially, and so were the Abbotts. "Just an idea," I said. "I'm an idea guy."

"More like an idea *goofball*," said Sandy.

"Whatever works," I muttered, except it wasn't exactly idea time. It was time-to-leave time, and they started to pack us all up. The class was counted to see if anyone was missing, and then everybody started back up the stairs. I was following when I felt that hand on my shoulder again.

"Hold up, boy."

Me and my big mouth. I was in trouble and knew it, but this didn't stop me from trying to talk my way out of detention. "I just asked questions, I just wanted to know more about this Arthur thing, and I didn't mean anything bad by it."

"Easy, we know," said Mrs. Abbott, backing her husband off and giving me some room. "Take it easy."

"Okay."

Sizing me up, Abbott said, "You've an interest in robots, don't you, lad?"

I thought about it and shrugged. "I like the idea of having a machine buddy around who could bail me out of trouble."

"A good buddy," said Abbott.

"Yeah."

"What about the best of buddies?"

"Huh?"

135

Abbott didn't explain, not just yet. He said, "It's just that you seem so interested, we want to show you a couple of things about Arthur that . . . well, most of the class wouldn't understand."

"Oh, yeah?" This impressed me, since I was never one of the smartest kids in class. Maybe I had a knack for this robot thing. Maybe I could wind up working for NASA someday myself. Maybe I'd invent something so radical that I'd get in a fight with the bigshots, too.

"And the real important fact is we need a favor from you."

"A favor from me? What do you need?"

Important point: when adults start asking favors of thirteen-year-olds, nothing real good can possibly happen.

The Abbots linked arms and walked me over, saying, "Let's look at Arthur first, give you the real scoop."

The real scoop. So they showed me the robot again, and I was still impressed. I even asked a question: "Why haven't you turned him on yet?"

Abbott answered thoughtfully, saying, "Because once he's switched on, he can't be switched off."

"Why not?"

"We didn't build him with an off switch, and we did it on purpose. We want him to be as human as possible, and think about it, Max; how would you like it if you had an 'off' switch and everybody knew where it was?"

Good point. I'd spend a lot of time 'off' and parked in the closet at home, I figured, especially when Mom was gone and Dad's basketball games were on.

"It's a question of system integrity," Abbott was explaining. "The new type of computer intelligence we've developed—the higher function brain—is in its early stages. Only certain frequencies of brain activity can be replicated. Adult brain waves won't work—that's why I or Mrs. Abbott can't be used. We need a boy, laddie, a bright boy to help us finish the experiment."

I was getting a cold, scary feeling now. "Uh . . . yeah, right," I said to Abbott and Mrs. Abbott, backing away as I spoke. "So what exactly is it that you guys want from me?"

It was the Mrs. who answered, and her smile made me shudder. "Max, we need to borrow your brain. . . ."

ABOUT THE AUTHOR

Novelist M.T. COFFIN, whose "Spinetinglers" novels have sold more than one million copies, began his career writing obituaries as a freelancer for his local newspaper, *The Nightly Caller*. This was in addition to his full-time job in the Dead Letter Department of the post office. While he thoroughly enjoyed writing about the dead, M.T. Coffin abandoned that work to begin his first novel when a series of nightmares so amused and delighted him that he felt he must write them down to share with his friends and family. He wrote thirteen "Spinetinglers" before his wife, Berry A. Coffin, convinced him that the stories were interesting and exciting enough to share with others and helped him to submit his manuscripts to Avon Books for possible publication. The books were accepted immediately and the "Spinetinglers" series was born when the first novel, *The Substitute Creature,* was published in March 1995.

Gwen Montgomery, of the Young Readers Department at Avon books, is delighted to be publishing M.T. Coffin and says, "My spine tingled on the very first page and I knew right then that M.T. Coffin's books would keep readers dying for more."

M.T. Coffin was born on October 31 in Death Valley,

California. The year is uncertain since, for some mysterious reason, all records of his birth except the date have disappeared, and no records of any family members have ever been discovered. Raised as an orphan, M.T. Coffin attended Death Valley High School. After graduation, he attended DeKay University where he studied literature. It was there that he was introduced to the works of authors who were to be among his lifelong favorites, including Bram Stoker, Mary Shelley, H. G. Wells, Jules Verne, Mark Twain, and Edgar Allan Poe. It was also there that he met Berry during a blood drive on campus. Berry received a Bachelor of Arts degree in elementary education from DeKay and today is a substitute teacher and bee keeper.

Now, M.T. Coffin is writing full-time and has just completed *Gimme Back My Brain.* Works in progress include *Your Turn—to Scream, The Curse of the Cheerleaders,* and *Wear and Scare.* He is currently traveling to research upcoming novels and has most recently visited Transylvania in Romania and Murderers Creek, Oregon. Other "Spinetinglers" by M.T. Coffin include *Billy Baker's Dog Won't Stay Buried, My Teacher's a Bug, Where have All the Parents Gone?, Check It Out—and Die!, Simon Says, "Croak!,"* and *Snow Day.*

M.T. Coffin lives in Tombstone, Arizona, with Berry and their two children, Phillip A. Coffin and Carrie A. Coffin, and their dog Bones. He enjoys many hobbies, including reading, collecting books, taxidermy, playing the pipe organ, and bug collecting, an activity the entire family enjoys. The Coffins split their time between Arizona and their summer vacation home in Slaughter Beach, Delaware.

When asked about "Spinetinglers" and his many readers, M.T. Coffin responds, "I get goosebumps every time I think about how exciting it is to be able to tell stories all the time, and to reach so many people. I plan to keep writing forever.'"